THE JOURNEY HOME

by Doreen Nelson

The Journey Home
Copyright pending by Doreen Nelson

This book is dedicated to
My Family....

To my brother
Who has always stood by my side.

I love you

Special Thanks

To my cousin Carol Baker Murray who I have recently reunited with after too many years to count. It is her research in genealogy that inspired me to write this book. We have discovered that we share the belief that there is nothing more important than family. ❤

You are not alone. You are a leaf among thousands of leaves born from the many branches of a deeply rooted tree.

Other Books by Doreen Nelson

Maternal Instinct:
A game of life and death

Born Behind the Veil

I'll Always Love You
Even After I Die

When Werewolves Howl

Capone
The American Pit Bull Terrier Ambassador

The Mean Gene

ONE

I'm a slight man in stature. Five foot eight, maybe nine if I don't walk slumped over. When I notice myself doing it, I correct my posture immediately. I did it more when I was younger. Highly respected. Even feared by some. Appropriately lean and toned for my height. I would be proud of my physique….if pride was a factor in my life. It would take someone who knew me way back when to appreciate the road I've had to travel, the things I've had to do, the sacrifices I've had to make….to get to where I am. I like to remember where I came from so that I can fully appreciate my life now. Although everyone's journey begins even before they are born, it was at the age of seventeen when I remember first embarking on my conscious pilgrimage through life.

In looking back, I'd been bounced around the foster system all of my life….until I turned eighteen at which point I was kicked to the streets with just the clothes on my back….and my Birth Certificate in hand which had an interesting story in and of itself.

At around the age of fourteen years, as I was being tossed from one foster home to the next, an African American Social Service Worker who went by the name of *Auntie Amne* was assigned to follow up on me after I was relocated to yet *another* foster home. She told me in confidence that my mother's name was Sarah. No last name. She was said to be a beautiful, naive, light skinned, blonde haired, blue eyed Caucasian southern belle from

New Orleans, Louisiana who at the age of fifteen years accompanied her missionary parents to the deepest parts of the forests in the country of Kenya in the continent of Africa to provide medical supplies and preach Christianity to one of the last known Waswahili tribes not yet affected by the Arabic influence. That's where she met and fell in love with my father, *Mfalme,* which in the Waswahili tribal language of Kiswahili means *King.* At the time, my father was a seventeen year old dark skinned African warrior of Waswahili origin and next in line to be the tribal Chief of his family's clan. If what *Auntie Amne* said was true, as I preferred to believe it was, then I was born with my mother's blonde hair color and blue eyes and my father's kinky hair texture and dark skin....and the royal blood of an African Waswahili Chief.

The story went that Sarah became pregnant while on that mission with her parents to Kenya's remote forests....with me. Once they learned of the pregnancy, they packed their underage daughter up and leaving *Mfalme* behind, traveled back to the United States where she was conveniently stashed away in a home for unwed pregnant women who were giving their babies up for adoption. When potential parents interviewed her, she defiantly told them her baby's father was an African Chief. Since it was a time when nobody wanted to take on the task of raising a biracial child, when Sarah gave birth I was wrenched from her arms and placed into the foster system. The one thing she insisted on before signing me over to the authorities was that I be given the African Waswahili first name my father picked for me....*Chacha....*which means *Strong* *man.* When coupled with what I supposed was my father's tribal family name of *Boro,* my full name became *Chacha Boro.* I was told by another Social Service Worker that my mother committed suicide at the age of sixteen....shortly after my birth. It was said that her love was so strong for my father and her heart so broken over having to give me up to the foster system that she could not bear going through life without us. So it came to be that the name *Chacha Boro* was boldy and permanently typed across the face of my Birth Certificate accompanied by the official raised Seal of Louisiana attesting to its legality.

So with the clothes on my back and Birth Certificate in hand at the age of eighteen I began my life of freedom. Not having anywhere to go and no money to feed myself, I picked out a vacant corner on a busy street in the French Quarter in the city of New Orleans, sat myself down, placed a tin can in front of me, and began to sing one African Waswahili song after another. Having made it a point to learn the language of Kiswahili fluently, I was able to sing and dance to the slower beat of Taarab music as well as the faster tempo of Chakacha music.

The streets of the French Quarter in New Orleans were filled with tourists as well as locals who danced, drank, laughed and ate while celebrating the various festivities of each month which included the likes of the Mardi Gras, the Jazz Fest, the French Quarter Fest, the Running of the Bulls and many others. Multitudes of people were either sitting at the restaurant outdoor patios or walking around with alcohol to-go cups and plates of cajun food, crawfish, gumbo, krewes, king cake, and oysters.

New Orleans is a city that celebrates life. Even panhandlers, like me, are able to claim a street corner and earn a modest income. But you could not be lazy. You had to offer something unique to those who traveled so far to enjoy the festivities and parades in New Orleans....if you wanted to make any money, that is.

Across the street from *my* corner, my eyes were drawn to a store called *"Bibi's Oddities and Curiosities."* I knew *bibi,* pronounced bee-bee, was Kiswahili for *grandmother.* In the display window sat a Waswahili tribal drum. Crouched down over the drum, with his hands posed as though he were playing it, was an African male mannequin around whose waist hung a red *shuka* cloth and beneath that, covering his genitals, a cowhide loincloth. A *shuka* cloth was worn by Waswahili warriors to be tied to drape across and around different parts of the body. This particular mannequin wore it tied around his waist, then the material was double flapped over to secure its position so that it would not drag on the ground when walking.

I began to fantasize about living in Africa with my father where I was sure I would have been treated like royalty....and wouldn't have had to shave my head to hide my kinky blonde hair. In the Waswahili peoples eyes, I would have been worshipped for what modern Western civilization ridiculed. I was told that my father was a descendant of a long line of Waswahili African Chiefs dating back to the beginning of time. With a far away look in my eyes, I often pictured myself running alongside my father through the forests of Kenya as we hunted, built tribal shacks, and ate from the nourishment that the land

14

provided us. Perhaps, if my mother's parents would have allowed her to stay with *Mfalme*, I, *Chacha Boro*, would have by now been Chief of my Waswahili ancestors' tribe....or at the very least next in line....after my father. I wondered if I had any Waswahili half sisters or brothers.

Even though I never met my father, I loved and respected him. I saw him as a proud man. Handsome. Strong. A leader of men. I was told that my tribal family was among the last to follow an ancient religion called *Animism*. They believe all people and animals have different degrees and amounts of power called *mana*. It is also their belief that certain plants, trees, and even rocks can possess *mana* and that different spirits can overtake one's body....sometimes good, sometimes bad. *Mulungu* is the highest spirit worshipped. He is equal to what Christianity calls *God* and the Muslims call *Allah*. Because of his high status, however, he never deals directly with a person. Instead, he sends another person, or a plant, or an animal with whatever *mana* he deems necessary to solve the problem.

At the time, I was sure my father had risen through the ranks and bore the title of Waswahili Chief. I imagined him being carried everywhere so that his *mana* would not be absorbed by others who might walk on top of his footsteps. I knew this to be true because I spent the better portion of my young life studying the ancient African Waswahili people and their ways.

When I sat down for the first time on the corner that I claimed as mine to go about the business of earning a living in the busy city of New Orleans, my mind began to

15

wander. I have a secret. No one knows about it but me. It isn't something I can share with anyone else. The foster mother I was living with at the time said she first noticed a change in me at the age of seventeen years old.

"As a matter of fact, *Chacha*," I recall her saying in that irritatingly testy southern accent, "it was when we were drivin' home from your dental appointment one hot and stormy Monday afternoon in the summer month of June. It was pourin' down rain. One of the worst lightnin' storms in Louisiana history."

"Yes," I remember thinking to myself as I grabbed a towel to wipe the sweat from my face and shaved head as the hot Louisiana sun shone down on me, *"That's exactly how I remember it, too."*

Some people, if they knew about it, would have called it a gift....perhaps from *God*....but I knew better. I chose to think of it as a SuperPower. A force of global proportions given to my dentist, *Dr. Nnamani,* to pass on to me by the Waswahili God....*Mulungu*. This particular visit was the first time I ever met *Dr. Nnamani*. The Social Worker, *Auntie Amne,* who secretly told me about my lineage set the appointment up.

"Yes," I thought to myself, *"I am sure it was Dr. Nnamani who was sent to bestow upon me a gift that would change the course of my life."*

Taking a break from my thoughts to hopefully hear the clink of a coin, or coins, hitting the bottom of my empty tin can, I stood to chant an African Waswahili song as a group of tourists stopped ever so briefly to listen. *clink, clink, clink, clink, clink*. As they walked away, I sat back down and slugged down a gulp or two of a bottled water one of the shop owners gave me.

"The shop owner across the street," I mumbled enviously aloud. "The shop that has displayed in its window the Waswahili tribal drum, red *shuka* cloth, and cowhide loincloth."

She was an older dark skinned woman. A little on the plump side. A very wrinkled face which I was sure each deep furrow represented a blessing or sadness in her life. She wore a mumu type dress that bore bright red and yellow colors. On her head sat an equally brightly colored sun hat.

"She looks like she could be someone's grandmother," I remember thinking to myself.

She always had a smile on her face….but there was something about her….something I couldn't quite put my finger on.

Getting back to my thoughts of that day at the age of seventeen as I sat in the chair in *Dr. Nnamani's* dental office, it suddenly occurred to me that oddly the dentist was Waswahili, too. Since I was well versed in all of the traditions, language, lifestyle, and religion of the Waswahili people, I knew this to be true because, besides bearing a Waswahili family last name, on the wall hung a Waswahili Medicine Man Mask. When I asked *Dr. Nnamani* about it, he whispered to me that he had the powers of a Waswahili Shaman passed down to him from his father and his father's father and his father's father's father, etc. etc. etc. After that, every time I had a dentist appointment, *Dr. Nnamani* would turn my chair to where I could see the

17

Medicine Man Mask staring at me from where it was evenly and with great pride hanging in the middle of the wall that sat directly in front of me. I had to admit that even though I was of Waswahili blood, it gave me the heebee jeebees. I knew that tribal Medicine Men had great powers and could even transcend their own bodies in order to accomplish a blessing or a curse.

Jumping up to sing another African Waswahili song to a crowd of passersby, I recalled that last fateful trip to the dentist as I sat in the chair gripping its arms until my knuckles turned white and holding my mouth open so wide I thought my jaw would break. One of my decaying back molars needed tending to *again*. *Dr. Nnamani* said the only option was to pull it. I remembered him humming a hypnotizing little tune that I was sure would be complete if the sounds of the tribal drum were added.

"As a matter of fact," I said to myself as a crowd of people gathered around me, *"today is a perfect day for such a tune."*

To take the place of the tribal drums, I slapped and clapped my legs and knees with my open hands. Closing my eyes, I envisioned that day as I sat in that chair on the third floor of the poorly maintained building where *Dr. Nnamani* conducted his business of Dentistry. It was a hot day. Humid. Pouring down rain. Dark skies. Thunder clouds. Lightning.

The stormy weather at least took my mind off of the fact that *Dr. Nnamani* was sticking a 27 gauge extra long needle attached to a 20 cc syringe filled with lidocaine over and over again into the inside of my mouth. His test as to the degree of numbness accomplished was when water involuntarily came pouring out of my mouth as I tried to drink from a small cup of water. I imagined it to be a modern day Waswahili Rite of Passage into manhood as I willed myself not to flinch or scream.

Suddenly my thoughts were interrupted by the sound of coins dropping into my tin can....*clink, clink, clink, clink, clink, clink, clink, clink, clink, clink, clink*....as the crowd walked away I stopped singing, emptied the coins into a worn backpack I found in a garbage dumpster, then placed the now empty tin can back down in front of me before the next wave of patrons came along. Returning to my thoughts, I heard *Dr. Nnamani's* voice echo through my mind.

"This will take only a minute or two." I recalled him saying as he wiped the water from my chin, neck, and chest. "Bear with me. You're going to walk out of here with a whole new outlook on life."

Just then, at that very moment, a bolt of lightning shot through the open window on the third floor of that poorly maintained building striking the drill that *Dr. Nnamani* was holding in his hand as well as the tooth he was working on. Dropping the drill to the floor, *Dr. Nnamani* began to twitch uncontrollably as I joined him in what could have been misinterpreted as a tribal dance to rid one's body of evil spirits. When we were all done gyrating, him on the floor and me in the chair, *Dr. Nnamani* stood, brushed himself off as though nothing happened, extended his hand to me and, once confident I was steady on my feet, he walked out the door mumbling something that sounded like he would reschedule me. Curiously, in his hand he had tightly clutched….my bloody back molar.

One thing I was quite sure of that day was when the dentist took me by the hand to help me from the chair, the eyes of the Waswahili Medicine Man mask glared a bright red at exactly the same time that an ever so brief final electrical shock shot from *Dr. Nnamani's* hand through mine. It only lasted a second….or two.

All I knew was that before I met with *Dr. Nnamani* on that hot and stormy Monday afternoon, I was a below average Joe. Nothing special about me. My grades weren't even good enough to get me into a Community College….as my *too many to count* foster mothers constantly reminded me. A "low achiever" is what they called me. I didn't have the ambition or energy to try any harder than the half-assed efforts I'd been making all of my life. All through my growing years I was on the heavy side….No, I was fat. The only thing that changed about me when I began my teen years was that I developed a bad case of acne. I seldom bathed. Never washed my hair which at one time looked like I stuck my finger into an electrical socket. I wore thick black horn-rimmed glasses. Frequent trips to the dentist all of my life were the result of a lackluster routine of brushing my teeth. No friends. Was bullied a lot. Wore too small to fit hand me down clothes. Was made fun of by both the white and black kids for being biracial. They taunted me by calling me…."Whack."

Putting two and two together, I came to the conclusion that the *"wh"* stood for white and the *"ack"* stood for black…. *"Whack."*

It didn't take a rocket scientist to figure it out....especially when they taunted me with the song they made up about me....

"Whack, Whack
Half white Half black
He's so fat
You can see his butt crack"

The neighborhood girls even jumped rope singing it.

"Well," I smiled to myself, *"Dr. Nnamani was right about one thing. My life certainly made a dramatic change after that visit to his office at the age of seventeen."*

The very next day after that life changing event, I began running. Put myself through grueling daily workouts with and without weights. Lost over a hundred pounds in no time. Started brushing my teeth, sometimes three times a day. Took a shower every night before bed. That's when I decided to shave my head as close to the scalp as possible without making it bleed, then took a bath towel and some oil and polished it like one would a shoe. Kept my nails clean and well-trimmed....fingers and toes. For whatever reason, I didn't need to wear glasses anymore. Went to the library every day to absorb whatever knowledge I could about the Waswahili people and the world in general. I immersed myself into the religion called *Animism* and started praying to the Waswahili African God *Mulungu.*

After what I'd come to call *the Mulungu miracle,* I visited *Dr. Nnamani* often. Unfortunately, he didn't fare as well as I did. He now sat in a wheelchair in a Home for the Mentally Disabled wearing that Waswahili Medicine Man Mask while drooling and mumbling the same words over and over again….

"Hauko peke yako"

Which when translated into English meant….

"You are not alone."

From a colorful twine around his neck hung my back molar….along with it were strung many other teeth in various sizes and shapes.

On my eighteenth birthday, my first stop after leaving the foster home was to visit *Dr. Nnamani.* He was sitting slumped over in his wheelchair in his usual place in the large room filled with many of the other residents and their visitors at the Home for the Mentally Disabled.

This time, when I approached him and before I had a chance to say anything, he stood from his wheelchair, held his head up high while straightening his posture, then after removing that necklace of teeth from around his neck, he leaned over to place it around my neck. Grasping my right hand in his left, he held onto it tightly as his eyes behind the Medicine Man mask glowed red and a bolt of electricity once again shot through my body. Before slumping back down into his wheelchair, he said one last time….

"Hauko peke yako."

When I came back the next week to visit him, I was told he went to live with his family. Even though I felt sad at the thought of never seeing *Dr. Nnamani* again, the *mana* of the teeth hanging around my neck gave me a feeling of pride and a renewed hope. I didn't feel so alone anymore.

TWO

So it was, day after day, I sat at *my* corner from nine in the morning until two the next morning. On weekends, I stayed later. After my final visit with *Dr. Nnamani,* I decided to save my money, after food of course, to one day take a trip to one of the deepest, darkest parts of Africa....I wasn't quite sure where yet. It became my dream to one day meet my father....*Mfalme.*

So I sang....and I sang....and I sang. After teaching myself a Waswahili tribal dance, I began to hop around and move my feet all the while clapping and slapping my legs and knees with my hands while singing one Waswahili song after another. I put every ounce of energy I had into my performance. My life depended on it. As I danced, I often felt my body transcend to a far away place and time leaving my physical self behind to carry on the responsibility of entertaining my audience while high up into the skies I soared, through the forests I ran, and up the mountains I climbed. By my side ran the likes of elephants, lions, zebras, and giraffes. When my song and dance ended, I felt my spirit being sucked back into my physical body as I collapsed to the ground on my knees, then in one last attempt to hold onto the places I'd just been, I'd throw my head back and howl as a wolf would when announcing to the world that he was a power to be reckoned with. When my howling stopped, in its place, increasing in volume and intensity, the deafening applause of people surrounding me filled my ears. Not only was there the clinking of coins hitting the bottom and sides of the tin can that sat loyally in front of me but the soft flutter and flow of dollar bills being tossed were overflowing as well onto the concrete. As soon as one group of people left, another would take their place. And so it was that day after day and into the night I not only danced and sang but transcended to a place I'd never been but knew I was destined to one day go.

Then, one day out of the blue, the old woman who owned the store directly across the street from my corner who went by the name of *Bibi* came walking across the street towards me. In her arms she carried that Waswahili tribal drum I'd admired for so long. When she reached me, she set it down next to me and grabbed a coin out of my tin can.

"Asante" she said, which in Kiswahili means "Thank you."

Without another word, she walked back across the street to her store.

I couldn't believe that the Waswahili tribal drum that I admired for such a long time that sat in the display window in the store across the street from my corner now belonged to me. As I danced and pounded on the drum to match the beat of whatever African Waswahili song I chose to sing for the passersby, I felt the happiest I'd ever been. Coin after coin, dollar after dollar was dropped into and around my tin can. I soon realized that since my acquisition of the drum, I was emptying my tin can far more often than I ever had before. I took very good care of my drum and believed it contained a good spirit.

A few months later, I watched as *Bibi* once again made her way through the heavy traffic to cross the street to where I sat. This time she was carrying the red *shuka* cloth and cowhide loincloth in her arms. When she reached me, she motioned for me to stand, took that red *shuka* cloth and tied it around my waist, then flapped the material over two times. It was the very same one that I admired for so long that the African male mannequin wore as he sat crouched over playing the tribal drum in the display window of *Bibi's* store. After securing it around my waist, she handed me the cowhide loincloth and pointed to my genitals. She then took two coins from my tin can.

"Asante." she once again said before turning to walk away. This time she smiled.

I learned to play that tribal drum as though I was born to it. I imagined myself as a child sitting next to my father, *Mfalme,* being taught the ways of the tribe. When I closed my eyes, I felt myself going into a deep trance. When my song ended and my eyes opened, my tin can was overflowing with even more coins and dollars. So it came to be that with the necklace of teeth hanging around my neck, the red *shuka* cloth around my waist, and the cowhide loincloth beneath, I sang, danced, and played the tribal drum while the *mana* of the spirits sent to me by the god *Mulungu* shot through my hands, body, and feet. The motion of the necklace made of teeth swung gracefully across my bare chest to the beat of the music. In the distance I could hear the sounds of coins hitting the sides and bottom of my tin can....*clink clink clink clink clink clink clink clink clink clink clink clink clink.*

A few weeks after *Bibi* presented to me the red *shuka* cloth and cowhide loincloth, I walked across the street to her store to drop off my too small to fit hand me down clothes….including my shoes. Having folded them neatly, I handed them over to *Bibi* saying,

"Kwa mtu aliye ha uhitaji"

Then followed with,

"For someone in need."

Looking down at my now bare feet, she ran to the back of the store and returned with a pair of leather sandals that fit my feet perfectly. With that, *Bibi* smiled and grasped my hand passing a coin from her hand to mine. Before letting go, she said,

"Hauko peke pako. Una jani kati ya maelfu ya majani mtoto kutoka matawi mengi ya mti linafanyika."

I smiled at the old woman knowing what she just said to me….

"You are not alone. You are a leaf among thousands of leaves born from the many branches of a deeply rooted tree."

For the first time in my life, I felt as though I belonged to something greater than myself. I no longer felt alone. My desire to find my father….my family….began to take over my every move, my every word, my every action, my every thought.

Clutching the coin in my hand, I bowed to *Bibi,* then before walking away, I said,

"Asante….Thank you."

Bibi smiled at me as she stood at the doorway waving goodbye and I turned to walk back across the street to my corner.

Looking at the shiny gold coin given to me by *Bibi,* I knew I'd seen it before….in a book?….at the library? Deeply imprinted into one side of the coin was an African man dressed in Waswahili tribal attire. At his feet sat a tribal drum….

"Just like the tribal drum Bibi gave me," I thought to myself.

On the other side of the coin were the chiseled words *Kenya, Africa.*

That night as I lay in the small section of the alley I claimed as mine, I began to dream….

I watched myself walking barefoot through a forest of trees while clad in the red shuka cloth given to me by Bibi now tied around my shoulder and draped down across the front and back of my body. Around my waist, I had cross-tied my drum. Around my neck, I wore the necklace of teeth given to me by Dr. Nnamani. I was no longer bald. Instead, on top of my head sprung sproutings of the kinky textured blonde hair I was born with. I wore it proudly for all to see. In the distance, I saw the glare of the red eyes of the Waswahili Medicine Man mask beckoning me. Alongside me walked an elephant. Suddenly the gold coin bibi gave me dropped from my hand and rolled to the front door of a Museum located in Kenya, Africa.

When I woke the next morning, I knew what I must do. *Mulungu* had spoken to me in my dream. Packing up what little I had in the way of possessions, I decided to say goodbye to the store owner, *Bibi,* who had given me so much. When I arrived at my corner in the city of New Orleans, I crossed the busy street to walk over to *"Bibi's Oddities and Curiosities"* store. This time when I walked into the store, there was a Caucasian southern speaking lady waiting on customers. When I inquired as to the whereabouts of *Bibi,* I was told she left that morning to visit her grandchildren in Africa.

I knew immediately that this was the work of *Mulungu* guiding me in the direction I must travel. It was then that I decided to begin my journey. Looking at the coin given to me by *Bibi,* I tossed it into the air. When it hit the ground, the side with the chiseled words *Kenya, Africa* settled itself face up.

THREE

With my backpack filled with the money I saved from the day I took custody of my corner on my eighteenth birthday one year ago to now, the tribal drum cross-tied around my waist, the necklace of teeth hanging around my neck, the red *shuka* cloth tied at my shoulder causing it to drape down to cover the front and back of my body along with the cowhide loincloth beneath, the leather sandals on my feet, and the coin *Bibi* gave me clutched tightly in my hand, I began my journey to Africa.

I hoped to find a cargo ship at the Port of New Orleans whose destination was Port Mombasa, Kenya. I learned in my first year of freedom that everything in life must be earned and thanks given to those who provided me with the means, opportunity, and knowledge to move forward. I did not want any bad *mana* invading my life. So it was, each night when I closed my eyes to sleep, I gave thanks to the Waswahili god *Mulungu* for sending the spirits meant to guide me by using the bodies of the Social Worker *Auntie Amne, Dr. Nnamani,* and *Bibi.*

In just two years, from the age of seventeen, I had changed so much. Not only physically but spiritually as well. I now realized that for the first seventeen years of my life, I concealed my real self from those who made fun of me, looked at me differently, or called me *"Whack."* It was now time for me to walk confidently in my own skin and be who I was born to be. But who was I born to be? I was sure the answer lay in my ancestry. I knew I must find my

Waswahili family. In remembering *Bibi's* words, I set out to locate *"all of the other thousands of leaves that were born from the many branches of my deeply rooted family tree."* It was then that I threw my razor away and decided to allow my blonde kinky hair to grow out. After all, my mother had as much to do with my beginning as my father. To ignore any part of my roots would be disrespectful. I never felt so alive and in touch with the world.

I started out for the Port of New Orleans. I was confident that the smell of the Atlantic Ocean waters and the loud clanging, grunting sounds of cargo boat engines would tell me when I was near my destination. In preparation for my journey, I began cutting my food rations down to once every other day being careful to buy only those foods that didn't rot easily or carry an odor about them. I read that the purchase of plastic seal proof baggies would provide me an odorless place to store my defecation. My plan was to hide in the freefall lifeboat that was attached to the rear of the cargo ship. I'd spent a lot of time at the library researching the best way to successfully stow myself away on a cargo boat. I would prefer to offer my services in exchange for free passage and food but I didn't have the documents or training necessary and it would take too long of a time to obtain everything needed to even work in the most menial of positions aboard the craft.

The cargo boat I intended to stow myself away on was one that would begin its departure from the Port of New Orleans then take the sea route traveling through the Gulf of Mexico, the Straits of Florida, the North Atlantic Ocean, the Strait of Gibraltar, the Alboran Sea, the

Mediterranean Sea, the Damietta Branch River, the Nile River, the Ismailiya Canal River, the Suez Canal, the Suez Canal River, the Gulf of Suez, the Red Sea, the Gulf of Aden, the Arabian Sea, the Indian Ocean, and finally make its landing at the Port of Mombasa, Kenya. It was 10,764 nautical miles from New Orleans to Kenya. At 10 knots/hour, we would arrive at our destination in approximately forty-five days. The boat was to set sail from New Orleans in five days. I realized I would have to lay very still in the mostly enclosed freefall lifeboat so I would not be discovered. No sneezing, snoring, or even heavy breathing. I heard that if I was caught while at sea, the Captain of the ship would most likely cast me into the turbulent ocean waters on a flimsy makeshift lifeboat made of two logs and one huge empty hollowed out oil drum in the middle. The only other option he would be left with would be to make me a prisoner of the ship under lock and key, then turn me over to the authorities when we landed. The problem with that was that the Owner of the ship would be fined many stiff penalty fees which in turn would amount to such an expense that it would cost the legal workers aboard the ship their jobs. It was just easier and less expensive to set the stowaways to sea and leave them to their own devices. Most of them would die at sea never to be heard from again.

Once I arrived at the Port of New Orleans, I was amazed at how vastly enormous a cargo carrier ship was. Locating the cargo boat that was setting sail for Mombasa Kenya in just a few days, I ran around to the rear of the boat and was able to catch a glimpse of the freefall lifeboat stored on a downward sloping slipway. It was bright orange in color and, except for its two narrow front windows, a mostly encapsulated steel vessel. This was going to be where I was going to live, hopefully undetected, for forty-five days….barring any sea storms or attacks by pirates that might lengthen our time at sea. The Gulf of Aden was well known for the antics of pirates who would find a way to scale the boat in order to either rob it of whatever cargo and monies it might be carrying to sell on the black market or to hijack the crew members and hold them for ransom….usually the latter of the two.

That night I went shopping for water, plastic seal proof baggies, and a limited amount of non-perishable food, all of which I would have to ration so that it would last for the forty-five day duration. I needed to be able to carry on board in one trip everything needed for my survival.

As luck, or destiny, would have it, I ran into a deckhand that worked on the very ship I was soon to sail. I was in the grocery when I overheard him speaking to another African man. They were not speaking English. Fortunately for me, they were speaking Kiswahili. The deckhand was in dire financial straits as he had gambled and lost two hundred American dollars aboard the boat he manned last trip. He was afraid to go home to face his wife and three children. They counted on his earnings for the necessities in life such as food, water, clothing, and a roof over their heads. I stepped up to the counter with my bottled water and asked the man in Kiswahili if he would like to make some money. He became overjoyed at the prospect of being able to recoup the money he lost so I took him aside and told him I would pay him the money he lost in gambling if he would help stow me away in the freefall lifeboat. We made arrangements to meet at midnight the night before the ship was to set sail for the Port of Mombasa, Kenya. The deckhand told me that there were not only less people around at night but the last emergency practice for the workers utilizing the lifeboat was set for the afternoon before. It would not be checked again until just before they were to depart from the Port of Mombasa in Kenya to return back to the United States. He further advised me that when we reached our destination to disembark the ship by jumping off into the Indian Ocean when we were just a few hundred feet from shore so that I would not be discovered. For a little bit more money, he would knock on the lifeboat door three times when we were at the point that I should jump ship. Arrangements were then made for me to pay him half of the money now and the rest when we arrived at Port Mombasa.

Spending the next two nights in an alleyway I was not accustomed to, I dared not close my eyes to sleep and risk the possibility of being robbed. On the designated night I was to meet up with the deckhand at the boat at midnight, we stealthily made our way to the rear of the boat. He helped me carry my water and food aboard. Climbing up a ladder secured to the side of the boat in the rear, we made our way to the main level, and then climbed two additional sets of exterior stairways that led us to the back door of the lifeboat. Since it was slanted downwards so that in an emergency evacuation the nose of the lifeboat would hit the water first when the overhang was pulled, I would position myself at the most extreme angle in the pointed front portion on the floor.

Once settled in, the deckhand warned me to not make a sound or move in any way that may draw attention to the lifeboat. He said if I was discovered, he would deny any knowledge of me. My heart was racing as I sat cramped on the floor of my new quarters. It was now one in the morning. In four more hours my journey across the world would begin. My head was overcome with thoughts of meeting my family. I gave thanks to *Mulungu* for sending this deckhand my way and filling him with the *mana* needed to assist me in my journey.

The fact that I was expecting a quiet, calm, worry free trip proved what little I knew about the sea and the men who traveled it.

FOUR

I fell asleep for an indeterminate amount of time nestled as snugly as a fetus in its mother's womb although not as comfortably being that the womb I lay in was made of steel. I was suddenly awakened by the loud blasting of the ship's horn warning other boats of its departure. I could smell the brine in the ocean as we left shore. The cool dampness of the early morning hours caused the boat to shake and shudder a bit as one might do when first waking in the morning. I didn't need to open my eyes for all of my other senses to awaken in varying degrees of preservation. It was then that I realized it is the body's natural duty to protect itself in other ways when one of its sentries is disabled. I wondered if a blind man's sense of smell was stronger than those who were able to see. I was glad the deckhand thought to arm me with a *mkuki*, a sharply pointed wooden spear, he carved from hand. I was even more happy that I previously trained myself in the use of a similar weapon in the many ways of the ancient Waswahili….hunting, ceremonial rites, and battle. I wanted my father to be proud of me. The deckhand said if we were attacked by Somali Pirates at the Gulf of Aden and I was discovered, besides my hands and feet I would have no other means of protection. I felt I had made a friend of this man, tall in stature, long hair tied in varying lengths of braids, leathery black skin thickened from the sun and too many days at sea. An ear to ear smile allowed all to see his somewhat displaced and crooked surprisingly whiter than most teeth. He was a handsome man, albeit imperfect as all men are in one way or another. He stood with a straight back and by doing so attained his maximum height which was at least four inches taller than me. That is when I decided that when I reached the shore of my destination of Mombasa, Kenya and was freed from the crouched over cramped fetal position that was required of me now, I would no longer walk slouched over. I would present myself to the world, whether walking, sitting, or standing, with my head held high and back straightened to the umpteenth degree.

My new friend's name was *Jabari* which in Kiswahili means *brave one*. I felt he might be the fourth spiritual contact given to me by the God *Mulungu* for a successful journey.

As the cargo boat's heavy nomenclature chugged through the various waterways, I learned to differentiate between night and day not only by seeing through the small windows that sat at the front of the lifeboat pointing downward at the ocean but by the temperature changes as well. During the warmest time of the day, the sun beat down on the steel encapsulation that had become my living quarters. It was then that I would begin to sweat profusely. I found I was able to cool off some by shedding the *shuka* cloth draped around my mostly naked body. When night time came, I began to shiver so my *shuka* cloth was then used as a blanket to cover myself.

During the day, the ship was a busy place filled with the shouts and voices of the men working. In the early morning hours, I listened to the prayers of many a seafaring man as they privately knelt at the back of the boat giving thanks to their God of choice depending on their religion. I realized that even though the names of the Gods varied, the prayers were the same. Each man asking *his* God for a safe journey as well as the safety of his family back home. All of these men of different colors, nationalities, ethnicities, and religions bore one thing in common….they all believed in the spiritual power of a Higher Being. And so it was, with pencil in hand that I made the first entry in my seafaring journal….

"Since every human being is "born" with the innate "need" to worship an all knowing, all powerful, omnipresent Spiritual Being, so it must be that the proof of His existence, whether He goes by the name of Allah, God, Jehovah, or Mulungu, lies in the inherent microstructures of dna that exist in every living human being from birth since the beginning of time. Therefore, "God" is real. To find Him one must look inside oneself."

Each day I carved a notch into the steel wall of the lifeboat I lay prisoner in. I needed to keep track of my days. Not only would I be able to tell how many remaining days there were to travel but the even numbered days indicated when it was time for me to eat. Also, my friend, *Jabari,* warned me to be particularly observant of any unusual noises during the very early morning hours beginning on our thirty-seventh day at sea. These were the times we would be sailing through the dreaded waters of the Gulf of Aden where Piracy was rampant. He said that Somali fishermen turned Pirates were known to hijack a cargo boat in order to hold the Captain and crew ransom, demanding large amounts of money in return for their lives. The Pirates would approach the slow moving cargo boat while piloting a much faster moving skiff. In addition to bringing their own ladders to board the ship's stern at the rear of the boat, they would be carrying rapid propelled grenades and firearms. I planned on staying awake and alert from the moment I carved the thirty-seventh notch until we reached the Port of Mombasa, Kenya on the forty-fifth notch.

Jabari said he signed up for the midnight to four in the morning shift to act as look-out for the ship. During that time he might find a moment when he could release me for one or two minutes to stretch my limbs and pee over the side of the ship. This, too, would cost me extra. He said everyone would be fast asleep at around two or three in the morning so that was the time he chose. He told me not to worry if he didn't show up a night or two. It would just mean it wasn't safe for me to come out. I would pee into a plastic bottle container for all other times. I was glad I brought along with me, perhaps to fill my idle time, my notebook. I planned on writing in it my daily thoughts so that the boredom brought about by having to sit in the same encapsulated space for forty-five days might pass quicker.

Day One *On my first day at sea, I became quite nauseous from the tossing and turning of the ship in addition to the sound of the turbulent waves lapping powerfully against her sides. I was glad I brought more than enough seal proof baggies to cover the amounts of vomit as well as defecation thrust through one of the two exits of relief provided by my body. I hoped the loud thunderous sounds of the engines and clanging of the steel* bins carrying the cargo aboard this ship would override my sounds of human retching.

Jabari freed me from my confines for no more than two minutes. As we peed over the side of the boat together, he spoke of his family and his love for his wife, Banou (lady, princess,) and children, three boys named Mosi (first born), Kobe (Tortoise), and Barack (lightning, blessing).

Day Two. I shed my red shuka cloth from my body to accommodate the heat supplied by the midday sun. My stomach replaced the previous feelings of nausea with growling. My vomit having turned to bile sometime during the night was now reduced to an occasional gag. Quietly removing two cheese crackers, then adorning them heavily with the type of soft cheese that is easily and quietly emitted by the squeezing of the top of an unrefrigerated, air compressed spray can along with a two fingered swipe of peanut butter and a bottled water to wash it down, I ate my first of twenty-two meals.

At 2 am, Jabari and I peed over the side of the boat together while he told me of the hardships he and his family endured as the result of his being away from home for the duration of each boat's voyage.

Day Three I decided to do some reading. Although I previously had read the very same book I brought with me over and over again, I chose it to accompany me on my journey in case there was anything I may have missed. In detail, it told the story of the Waswahili people from ancient times to the present. I wanted to present myself at my best when I met my father, Mfalme. Besides there not being much natural light to read by, I had a hard time *staying awake as the boat lulled me to sleep as it rocked back and forth as a cradle might pacify a newborn baby.*

Jabari did not come to pee and talk with me this night. I miss him.

Day Four through Seven *I slept. On the even numbered days, I woke only long enough to prepare the two cheese crackers with the cheese spray and two fingered swipe of peanut butter topping along with a bottled water for my meal.*

On each night, Jabari brought a smile to my face with one of his seafaring tales....never forgetting to include talking about the antics of his three boys as well as the love of his life....his wife, Banou....whose beauty he compared only to the likes of the many mythic Black Goddesses of Africa.

Days Eight through Eighteen *Everything was fairly the same from one day to the next. I slept a lot. If it were not for the notches carved into the steel wall of the boat, I would have lost track of time.*

Jabari released me from my primate habitat long enough for me to pee each night. He told me that he had overwhelming feelings of loneliness and greatly missed his family. I could see the far away look in his eyes. Since he didn't have much to say, I thought perhaps I could serve to cheer him up a bit by telling him the story of The Tortoise and the Hare, knowing that one of his boys names meant Tortoise (Kobi) and the other Lightening (Barack). I don't know if he ever heard it before but his laughter indicated that my intention was accomplished. He grasped my hand and shook it just before he closed the door behind me....

"Asante rafiki yangu" he said....followed by *"Thank you, my friend."*

Day Nineteen *I acquired a friend, or so I thought, in the way of a very small mouse. Someone to talk to if nothing else, I thought to myself. Perhaps, he was sent to keep me company by the god Mulungu. When I noticed he was nibbling on a cheese cracker as he ran out through an ever so slight crack in the doorway, I hurriedly opened my once full box of crackers only to find most of them gone. All I had left to eat now were the remaining squirts of cheese from the spray can, a jar of peanut butter, and the bottled water. That night, I wondered....*

"There are those in this world who are much needier than others....perhaps, hungrier. Is it my obligation to feed all of my food to he who has nothing to eat if it means that by doing so I will starve?"

I thought long and hard for an answer pondering the mysteries of mankind and why we were the way we were. Before I came up with an answer, I fell back to sleep.

At two in the morning, Jabari came to wake me with much robust to my door. As we peed together, he told me he held his pee so that we might be able to talk longer. With a big smile on his face, he accounted to me how he had won one hundred american dollars in gambling this night. This was when I learned that Jabari's family did not live in New Orleans as I assumed but rather in Kenya, Africa. He was on his way home.

Day Twenty *Disoriented, I woke to the howling and shrill whistling sounds of a high velocity wind sweeping around and about the entirety of the boat. I was sure we were yet traversing across the North Atlantic Ocean. It wouldn't be until Day 23 that we would be embarking through the much calmer waters of the Sea of Gibraltar. I felt the lifeboat trying to violently free itself from its steel slanted containment as it shuddered and shook me back and forth. Grabbing onto the lifeboat steering wheel, I tried to brace myself as the ocean opened its mouth in an attempt to swallow the entire ship and all aboard. The waves must have been massively gigantic swells of water as I heard them pounding into the port (left) and starboard (right) sides of the boat while thrusting any excess water over onto the main deck where sat twenty-five tons of forty foot long steel bins. It was hard to understand what the crew members were shouting through the deafening claps of thunder. The tones of their voices escalated between fear and excitement. I knew that if this ship sank into the depths of the North Atlantic Ocean it would not be due to the inadequate efforts or inexperience of the crew aboard. I concentrated for a while on listening for my friend Jabari's voice in an attempt to block out the sounds of nature's wrath. Mulungu is one not to be ignored, however, as intrusive pictures of a dark sky with grey angry clouds lurking above an even darker tumultuous ocean with an impressively large cargo boat battling to survive massively high whitecap waves kept interrupting my attempts to concentrate on locating Jabari's voice. In my mind, I envisioned the image of a toy boat attempting to avoid the splashes of a child in a bathtub. The immensity and power of nature suddenly overwhelmed me and I puked. This time I believe it was more from fear than sea sickness. I prayed to the god Mulungu for my friend Jabari's safety. I hoped it was nothing I did to offend Mulungu.*

I did not expect Jabari to show this night for our nightly pee. I was right.

Day Twenty-One. *A continuation of Day Twenty.*

No Jabari.

Day Twenty-Two *I must have fallen asleep. Perhaps, to the lull of the waves in the aftermath of the storm. I woke up sweating. The sun must have been out. I removed my shuka cloth. I heard many of the crew workers shouting out to one another as they went about the business of repairing the damage done to the boat by the storm. I woke to the sounds of hammers pounding, loud voices hollering and laughing, drills buzzing, and the American flag flapping in the wind from a pole that reached up from the boat to the sky. I wondered if my friend, the mouse, fared as well as I did through the storm. I had a piece of cheese cracker left to eat from the meager scraps left to me. I took it and laid it out by the door to the cabin. Perhaps, as a peace offering....or human compassion for he who was born less than I? And now it occurred to me that this mouse who was not able to walk into a grocery and pick out what he wanted to eat for the day as man is capable of doing was forced to live off the land. He lives off of man....and whatever scraps he chooses to throw to him. He eats man's garbage....and occasionally a fresh box of cheese crackers. Is it not the responsibility of all mankind to nourish and nurture all of those not born with his capability and wit? I suddenly felt a deep sense of shame for having reduced my friend, the mouse, to having to resort to being a thief so that he might live. I prayed to the god Mulungu, not for His forgiveness of the mouse....but for mine.*

No sign of Jabari this night.

Day 23 *I learned a seafaring shanty I heard the crew singing early this morning and all through the day. Although it awakened me and caused me to remove my shuka cloth earlier than usual, in a weird sense, I felt I was out on the main deck singing along with them with the warm wind chapping my cheeks and a smile on my face. That's when I thought of how all of my life in the foster system I was deprived, whether by my own doing or not, of that ingredient that man needs most to grow and prosper....other people. The bonding that goes on between one man and another, woman to husband, child to father, friend to friend. Not to downplay the horrid effects of bullying, in many ways I now saw that I did nothing to stop it. I went through each day convincing myself that it didn't matter and for some reason somehow I deserved it. Instead of holding my head high and straightening my back, like my friend Jabari, I slumped over when I walked keeping my eyes to the ground. It was my choice not to brush my teeth, although I do believe that was Mulungu's way of forcing me to visit the Dentist, Dr. Nnamani. I often wondered after our brief encounter if he in fact really was a Dentist....or was he acting in his capacity as a Waswahili Medicine Man. I never saw any other patients in his office which seemed to be set up haphazardly in a condemned building. I chose not to bathe or wash my hair. It was my hand that delivered sweet after sweet into my mouth that not only caused me to gain an excessive unattractive unhealthy amount of weight but rotted my teeth as well. Thus, the name "Whack".... "Whack, Whack....Half white, half black....He's so fat....You can see his butt crack." I preferred to sing along with the crew than to recall such past embarrassing school yard ditties so I memorized the chorus part of the sea shanty "The Dead Horse," that the crew was singing and to myself I sang along with them....*

"A poor old man came riding by
And we say so, and we hope so (chorus)
A poor old man came riding by
Oh poor old horse (chorus).
Says I, "Old man your horse will die."
And we say so, and we hope so (chorus)
Says I, "Old man your horse will die."
Oh poor old horse. (chorus)

And if he dies we'll tan his skin
And we say so, and we hope so (chorus)
And if he don't we'll ride him again
Oh poor old horse. (chorus)

For one long month I rode him hard
And we say so, and we hope so (chorus)
For one long month we all rode him hard
Oh poor old horse. (chorus)

But now your month is up, old Turk

And we say so, and we hope so (chorus)
Get up, you swine, and look for work
Oh poor old horse. (chorus)

Get up you swine and look for graft
And we say so, and we hope so (chorus)
While we lays on and drags ye aft
Oh poor old horse. (chorus)

He's as dead as a nail in the lamp-room door
And we say so, and we hope so (chorus)
And he won't come worrying us no more
Oh poor old horse. (chorus)

We'll use the hair of his tail to sew our sails
And we say so, and we hope so (chorus)
And the iron of his shoe to make deck nails
Oh poor old horse. (chorus)

We'll hoist him up to the fore yard-arm
And we say so, and we hope so (chorus)
Where he won't do sailors any harm
Oh poor old horse. (chorus)

We'll drop him down with a long, long roll
And we say so, and we hope so (chorus)
Where the sharks will have his body and the Devil
take his soul.
Oh poor old horse." (chorus)

As my head bobbed side to side during the late evening (or) very early morning hours, it was hard to tell which, rap rap rap. It was Jabari! I jumped to my feet hitting my head on the ceiling of the steel lifeboat. Throwing my arms around him, I was thankful he survived the storm. He greeted me with his ever present and crooked happy smile. He apologized to me for not having come sooner but there was much work to be done aboard the boat as a result of the storm and many men were working through the night. As we peed over the back of the ship, he told me the tale of the storm and how one man died being dragged overboard by an enormous wave taller than the highest building. "We held a burial for him nonetheless," Jabari said, "by wrapping him in his blanket with his pillow tucked under his head and a picture of his wife in his pocket, we tossed him into the ocean so that he might sleep his eternal days and nights in comfort." Jabari told me the storm set us back a day so now it would be forty-six days to Port Mombasa. A better way to look at it was we were halfway there. "And we say so, and we hope so," I sang to myself.

FIVE

Day 24 *The heavy weight of the cargo ship seems to be enjoying a much smoother ride as it glides its way through the gently lapping waves of the water. I supposed that we had left the anger of the North Atlantic Ocean to enter into the calmer disposition of the Sea of Gibraltar. On its northern point lies Spain and on its southern lies Morocco. At its narrowest, Europe and Africa are separated by a mere 7.1 nautical miles, thus serving as a point of illegal immigration. I imagined the Rock of Gibraltar, in ancient times called the Pillars of Hercules, claiming its superiority over the waters by refusing to give up its stalwart position in even the worst of climates, settling its limestone bottom into the Straight's salty depths, and stretching its peak upward to bask in the beauty of the blue skies, perhaps, to seek refuge in the billowing of a white cloud....or two. Onward Onward, thought I, to the Alboran Sea and then, the Mediterranean Sea. A tidbit of knowledge ran through my mind as I recalled that five million years ago the Mediterranean Sea all but dried up leaving nothing but desert in its wake along with tons and tons of salt. This was due to the lands of Africa and Europe merging at a level above the Sea, thus, sealing the Strait of Gibraltar waterway which was the inlet by which the*

Atlantic Ocean kept the Mediterranean Sea replenished with water.

Day 25. The scrap of cheese cracker I set by the lifeboat door is gone. I hope my friend, the mouse, got it. He is probably hungry by now. I wonder if he has a family to feed. I know how important it must have been for him to find that morsel of food. When considering the size of mouse versus man, I imagine that scrap served to feed at least two or three of his kind. I believe that if there was not enough to go around, my friend, who I had come to call "Panya Rafiki" meaning "mouse friend" would forsake his portion. I began to think Mulungu sent him to teach me a lesson in humility and manners making him the fifth spirit to help me on my journey.

That night, I discussed with Jabari about the possibility of Panya Rafiki holstering a spirit sent from Mulungu to teach me a lesson. He quickly agreed choosing his words carefully so as not to inspire the wrath of a spirit. We cut our pee short that night. A couple of hours later, perhaps at the end of Jabari's shift around 4 am, I heard three soft knocks on the lifeboat door. When I opened it, on the floor lay a nice sized piece of cheese.

Day 26-36 Each day and night were pretty much the same. Smooth sailing, mild winds, calm waters. By the amount of sweating I was doing, I was sure the sun was bright and shining although the windows at the front of the lifeboat revealed nothing more than the rippling of shaded dark water. Even though Jabari said we were a day behind schedule, I decided to remain awake and alert on the thirty-seventh day to prepare for sailing through the Gulf of Aden....Pirate territory.

Jabari has gotten into the habit of not only bringing Panya Rafiki a piece of cheese each night but a small portion of his own dinner for me as well. I was appreciative for his kindness and began to think of a way to repay him for his generosity. After our two in the morning pee and more than welcome conversation, I returned to my claustrophobic habitat. Just as I sat after securing the doorway....rap rap rap Each night upon opening the door, I would find a piece of cheese and leftover rations for me from Jabari's dinner....minus Jabari. He expected no thanks from me....or Panya Rafiki.

Day 37 *Today is the day I must rise and wait. By wait I mean listen, pay attention, smell....be alert to the goings on outside of the lifeboat. We were either in or near Pirate Territory.*

When Jabari visited me for our 2 am pee, he warned me to keep my spear at the ready. We would be advancing through the Gulf of Aden on the morrow. We peed and after he went over the different ways to use the spear he gave me, he returned to his lookout position and I returned to my cowardly surrounding.

Day 38 *It must have been early morning. Not warm enough to remove my shuka cloth. I wondered if there was any hint of the sun. As I sat in complete silence, I heard in the distance the motor of a skiff....or two. As the sound of the motor(s) grew louder, I knew they weren't far off. Coming at a faster pace than the vessel I was traveling, I realized we would not fare well at any attempt to outrun* them. Then, all grew quiet. I figured the motors were turned off. I knew Jabari was either still on his shift or was in the process of turning his duty as lookout over to another crew member....the changing of the guards, if you will. Untying my red shuka cloth from my shoulder, I brought it down to my waist to tie it and then flap it over twice as a Waswahili Warrior would....Bibi's smiling face flashed through my mind. Knowing that most of the crew had not yet awakened to begin their seafaring duties....leaving only my friend Jabari, or his replacement, and a skeleton crew to protect the cargo boat from bow to stern from as many as perhaps fourteen pirates, I stealthily climbed as I imagined a ninja might from out of my state of captivity and rose to land on the main deck. Standing amongst the too many to count, piled one on top of another, steel bins reaching a height of perhaps twelve feet (or higher), I climbed to the top of one so that I might see better. Praying to the god Mulungu that He guide my feet, eyes, ears, and hands in the direction of the enemy so that I might help save this ship and her crew who had provided me with protection, albeit unknowingly, for the duration of my journey in my attempt to unite with my father, Mfalme. At that point, several bursts of lightning shot in rapid succession illuminating the dark starless sky and all aboard and beyond the ship as though in answer to my request. This time I would not drop my eyes to the ground nor would I ignore those who set out to capture or kill those aboard this ship. This time, I would stand tall and welcome whatever spirit was sent to take my body over. No one called "Whack" on board this ship! When I heard a *whisper and the ever so slight rattling of a ladder on the starboard side of the ship, I peered down from the height of the steel container that now served as my roost. Just as the top of a pirate's head appeared, with my back straightened, head held high, and spear raised to the sky, I jumped to my feet screaming in a high pitched witch-like demonic voice the first words that came to mind.... "PANYA RAFIKI!" At the same time, the unfortunate pirate attempting to scale the starboard side of the ship looked up at me, then fell backward into his skiff yelling as though the world was coming to an end.... "KUKIMBIA! NYEUPE NYWELE NYEUSI KUWALISHA PEPO!" which meant, "RUN! WHITE HAIRED BLACK SKINNED DEMON!" I must have been a sight to behold as lightning flashed all around me presenting to all the world what one would look like if he were standing in a dark room with the fluorescent lights flickering all about him. With racing heart and pounding pulse, I jumped twelve feet down to the main deck landing as a gazelle in graceful flight. Turning my head quickly to the left, I stopped long enough to hear the heavy banging of a ladder on the port side of the boat. Spear in hand, I rushed to disarm the pirate's hand carrying a gun that had presented itself first in his attempt to pull himself up to board the boat. Just as I heard the loud echoing sound of a gun being fired, from out of the shadows sprang Jabari. With the bullet headed in his direction, I threw myself through the air landing in front of my friend in time to take the bullet intended for him. I hit the ground with blood running down my arm. Within a moment's time, leaving a trail of blood, I climbed back to the top of the ship's cargo to watch the Pirates on both sides taking off at high speed in the opposite direction of our boat.*

Rushing back down to check on my friend, Jabari, I found gathered around him the other crew members dressed in nothing more than their underwear and hanging tightly onto various pieces of makeshift weaponry, such as canes, hairbrushes, and toiletry spray cans. As the Captain approached us, the crew stepped aside. I dropped to one knee placing my spear to the ground mentally preparing myself to learn how to navigate in a matter of minutes a lifeboat built out of two logs with an empty hollowed out oil drum in its middle. No matter how severely tortured, I would not confess to my friend Jabari's help. I was a stowaway. Few are hated more by seafaring Captains and crew. Instead, to my surprise, he laughed, commanded me to stand, then grabbed my hand and shook it. In turn, all the other crew members took their turns in shaking my hand for having saved their lives....including Jabari, who winked at me when we joined hands. I had gone from being a hated stowaway to a celebrated Warrior! I knew my father would be proud....as well as my mother.

Before I went to bed that night, my wound was tended to and I was allowed a shower. When I looked into the full length mirror, I did not recognize the reflection of the man looking back at me. He was emaciated with his ribs sticking out all along his front and sides, his smile and blue eyes had overtaken much of his black face leaving in its once somewhat handsome wake that of a demonic skeleton, and the kinky textured blonde hair that he once shaved to hide from the world who he truly was, had grown out from his scalp at least six inches forming a huge ball of hair around his head as well as an uncontrolled growth of kinky blonde hair on his chin, under his arms, and on his legs and chest. I couldn't help but laugh as I stared back at myself in the mirror. And now I understood what scared the Pirates causing them to flee and scream in their bantu language, "White haired black skinned demon!" Rather than shave my head and in order that I stay true to myself, I decided to wet my hair and braid it tightly against my scalp.

Although we were only seven days away from Port Mombasa, the Captain ordered me out of my hiding quarters so that I might eat and sleep with the crew for the remainder of our journey. He said he would make further arrangements for me to disembark the ship at a safe distance from shore so that I would not be caught by the Immigration Port Officials. That night, I slept the best I'd slept in the past thirty-eight days.

Day 39-45 For the next six days, I was taught the work of a deckhand. Amongst many other things, I scrubbed the deck, chipped and painted. I pulled my shifts, mostly alongside Jabari (at his request) including the midnight to four in the morning Lookout position he'd signed up for from the beginning. I was glad because we were still able to enjoy our two in the morning pee and conversation together.

I loved standing on the bow watching the boat as its pointed front sliced its way through the waters splashing an occasional spray of water my way, feeling the force of the warm wind hitting my face causing my cheeks to chap and redden, welcoming the heat of the sun shining down on my head. It occurred to me that these seafaring men were as close to their Higher Being as one could get. They were all dedicated and strong workers. Nature was all around me....Mulungu was all around me.

Day 46 *We were soon to arrive at the Port of Mombasa. The Captain decided to set me to shore in the lifeboat at the back of the boat that I'd laid concealed in the majority of my time on board this fine cargo carrying vessel. Since our arrival time was to be at six in the morning on this forty-sixth day at sea, Jabari instructed me in the piloting of the lifeboat. I was to leave it stranded on a designated sandy beach not far from Port Mombasa. It seemed rather simple and safe. At five in the morning, I bid farewell to Jabari, the Captain and his crew, and although he was nowhere to be found, Panya Rafiki. Steeling myself at the steering wheel, I fastened my seat belt as I prepared for the overhang to be released. So, with my red shuka cloth draped from my right shoulder to hang across my body and cowhide loincloth beneath, handcrafted wooden spear, Waswahili tribal drum, necklace of teeth, leather sandals, and Bibi's coin tightly grasped in my hand, I went shooting down into the warm tropical waters of the Indian Ocean safely encapsulated in the orange steel lifeboat that once served as my captivity and now served as my freedom.*

Six

When I navigated my way to the seclusion of the predesignated beach on the coastline of Mombasa, I banked the lifeboat so that it balanced itself atop the white sands as the ebb and flow of the tide rocked it from side to side. The Captain would be sending *Jabari* to pick it up on their way back to the Port of New Orleans. Not knowing where to go next, I decided to walk into the city of Mombasa. I knew it would not be easy to locate my father and his tribe.

Although I was accustomed to the hustle and bustle of city life, I was glad to see that there was an area in Mombasa called "Old Town" that somewhat stuck to their past culture and ways of life….if for no other reason than to make a living off of tourism. It is now a mixture of the Arab, Indian, and African cultures. Narrow cobblestone paved streets. Wooden balconies. Large curved decorative doors. The busy voices of traders and sellers. Some women were dressed in Muslim clothing, such as a *hijab* which is a scarf that covers the head while others wore either a sun hat or nothing to cover their hair. The men were the same….some wore a *kofia* which was a decorative cylindrical cap with a flat crown and others a baseball cap or no hat at all. Women were mostly attired in a blouse and an ankle length wrap around skirt while men wore jeans and t-shirts. In addition to English, everyone spoke Kiswahili or some broken but understandable form of both languages. The streets were loud and busy with car horns honking and disgruntled drivers with their heads hanging out their windows yelling. I decided to stop into a coffee shop in hopes of meeting someone who might be able to at least point me in the right direction.

I was waited on by a young African man around the same age as me. After ordering a cup of coffee, I asked if he might know someone who could assist me in finding my father. He pointed to an elderly man sitting alone at a small round wooden table on the patio outside. There were no umbrellas over any of the tables to serve as protection from the hot sun beating down on all who graced the restaurants that offered outdoor seating. I walked over to the old man asking if I might sit with him awhile. He eagerly nodded his head yes and motioned with one hand to the seat opposite his.

Taking a sip of my hot coffee, I decided to get down to what I wanted to ask him immediately.

"Do you know of the Waswahili people?" I asked

"Yeah," he answered in English with an African accent while pointing to himself. "Why do you ask? Are you a news reporter?"

"Have you ever heard of a Waswahili tribe living in the deepest parts of the forests in Kenya around twenty years ago who were not affected by the Arabic influence at the time?"

"I know many Waswahili people," he answered. "What tribe are you looking for and why?"

"My name is *Chacha….Chacha Boro*. I am looking for my father. My mother was a white woman from the United States. Her parents were Christian missionaries. She accompanied them on their missionary trip to the forests of

Kenya around twenty years ago in search of any tribes not yet affected by the Arabic Muslim faith. My father was amongst such a tribe. That's how my mother and father met. They fell in love and I was conceived. My mother was forced to return to the United States and to give me up to the foster system."

At first, the old man looked at me questioningly, as though he might not believe my story. Perhaps as a test of truth, he asked in Kiswahili,

"Nini jina la baba yako ni nini?"

"What is my father's name?" I repeated after him in English. "Jina la baba yangu ni *Mfalme,*" I answered in Kiswahili.

When his mouth opened up into a huge smile, I could not help but notice the yellowed and missing teeth in his mouth. His face was deeply wrinkled and his one hand shook every now and then. His forehead bore a scar that was shaped like the letter "R". His left eye was an opaque slime color probably indicative of blindness. The right eye was dark brown. He had gray kinky textured hair. Tall and thin. He had his right leg crossed over his left and he sat stooped over. At the ready, leaning up against his chair, was a walking cane. He was dressed in a pair of brown slacks and a blue button down shirt. On his head, he wore a wide brimmed straw hat. I found it odd he wore no shoes. On his left arm were three long lines laying at an angle. They looked like they had been put there by the slicing of a sharp knife.

"A tribal ritual?" I queried to myself.

Leaning over the table as much as his spine would allow, he said in confidence.

"*Mfalme!* I knew his grandfather, *Ohin (Chief)* long ago."

In my excitement, before he proceeded to tell me the story of my great grandfather, I excused myself, then ran to the counter and ordered two more *kahawas,* both black. The counter boy smiled at me for my use of the Kiswahili language in the ordering of coffee and threw in two sweet rolls.

Settling back down at the table, the old man introduced himself to me.

"Jina langu ni *Asani,*" he said grinning ear to ear. *"Rebellious!"* he proudly shouted as he raised his fist in the air.

I smiled back at him. Raising my fist in the air, I said "Jina langu ni *Chacha….Strong man!"*

Bringing our fists down to the table, one on top of the other, then gripping them together as one might do with a handshake, we both shouted….

"Waswahili brothers!"

Might I ask you why the letter "R" in the middle of your forehead? Is it some sort of tribal tattoo? Does it stand for Rebellious like your name?"

The smile disappeared from his face as he raised his shaking hand to rub softly over the hardened scarred skin tissue that formed the letter "R".

"No," he answered sadly, "It stands for "Runaway".

"Runaway?" I countered with a confused look on my face.

"Yeah," he said…."Mtumwa Mtoro!"

Then, as though mustering up the pride of his ancestors, he held his head up high, straightened his back as much as possible, and said,

"Runaway Slave."

SEVEN

When the old man pulled out the stub of a previously smoked cigar out of his pocket, I knew I needed to prepare myself for a very long story. I was excited to hear it. Unlike the children and young adults I attended school with throughout my lifetime, I had a tremendous amount of respect for the elderly. I realized that where they were I would one day be and that many of life's trials I had yet to travail they had already experienced and conquered. There was much to learn in their storytelling. In the tribes, if one is disrespectful to an elder, the punishment handed down by the Chief is harsh….ranging from blindness to death.

Lighting his cigar, he leaned back into the patio chair while struggling a bit for a comfortable position.

"You have to remember," he began, "I am one hundred one years old. Things that happened to me when I was young, do not happen anymore….at least not that anyone knows or talks about. My *kubwa babu kubwa (great great grandfather),* was brought over by boat from Africa to the United States to be sold into slavery. The *mmiliki mtumwa (slave owner)* who bought him, encouraged sexual relations between his slaves in the hopes that they'd produce more slaves for him. When I was born, I lived up to the meaning of my name in a short while of time. I was more than rebellious. I was angry. By the age of ten, I was planning my first runaway. I gathered together with three other slave boys on the plantation and we came up with a plan to escape. As we prepared to take off in the middle of the night, none of us got past the front door because each of our *babas (fathers)* were waiting on the porch with a belt in hand. After a proper ass whipping, my *baba* made me promise I'd never try to take off again. If I was caught by the *mmiliki mtumwa,* the beating would have been lots worse he said. Well, I was stubborn those days so when I turned thirteen, I decided to try again. This time, I went alone. I was on the run for seventeen days before I was caught and hauled back to the plantation. My punishment was getting beat real bad with a club on the bottoms of my feet."

Having said that, he lifted one of his feet up so I could see its bottom. Both were permanently swollen and scarred making it hard for him to walk with shoes on his feet.

"The letter "R" on my forehead" he continued, "stands for Runaway. They tied me to a tree so I was facing them. Two of them held my head in place, one on each side of me, then Master took a cattle branding iron and pressed it into my forehead until I could hear the flesh sizzling....like you'd hear when steaks are cooking on a grill is what I compared it to. While they had me where they wanted me, they topped the branding off by beating me in the eye with that club they used on my feet until I couldn't see no more. They said I was lucky they left me one good eye. I guess I'm thankful for that. I figured that was a good enough Rite of Passage into manhood for me since I didn't scream, cry, or move a muscle. After that, I kept on working that plantation alongside my *baba, mama,* and brothers and sisters. Never tried to run away again. Master was a black man. I don't think many people know that there were a lot of black men back in the United States who were slave owners. When Master died, his son took over the plantation and set all of his father's slaves free. My *mama* and *baba* were dead by then. I was nearly fifty years old. In my twenties, I coupled up with a slave woman but we never had any children. I'd pull out before any of my sperm could get in her. I didn't want to bring any offspring into the world that would have to be brought up as slaves. She died a year before we were set free."

A tear formed in his right good eye for one brief moment before he wiped it away.

Sitting up in his chair as straight as his crooked spine would allow, he took a sip of coffee which was long cold by now, then looked me straight on in the eyes.

"Mfalme!" he said. "You say you are his son?"

"Yes," I responded, "but I've never met him….or my mother. I was only given their names…. Sarah and *Mfalme."*

Pausing a moment, I thought to myself, *"Where are my manners?"* then offered my new found friend, *Asani*, a cold drink and a sandwich.

He eagerly took me up on my offer so while I ran up to the counter to order our drinks and food, he continued sitting at the table.

When I returned with two sandwiches, one for me and one for him along with two ice cold fruit drinks, he first took a bite of his sandwich then a quick sip of his drink.

"Sarah and *Mfalme,*" he continued. "Their story of love is well known around here."

So shocked was I by his words that my drink almost dropped from my hand.

"*Mfalme* was next in line after his father to be Chief of the family clan when he met Sarah. He was seventeen at the time. It is said their love for one another was one that could not be broken by any amount of distance or time. After Sarah was taken back to the United States, *Mfalme* became so distraught over the loss of Sarah and his baby that he went into a deep depression. His father, *Kondo* which in Kiswahili means *Warrior,* was a very brave and wise man. He refused to allow his tribe to become a part of the modern world….and that included the Christian missionaries. One night *Kondo* held a Rite of Passage for all the young men passing into manhood including his son, *Mfalme.* He figured the pain of circumcision would not only take his son's mind off of Sarah but in becoming a man he would grow stronger and the spirits would no longer allow him to feel the pain of a broken heart. So it was that *Mfalme* stood without expression, sound, or movement in front of the entire tribe as another adult male tribal member removed his foreskin with the sharp blade of a 12 centimetre knife without anesthetic. *Mfalme* had just turned eighteen. The last I heard of him, his father led his people beyond the forests of Kenya to escape the modern world and their beliefs including all Arabic influence and Christian missionaries. He believed *Mulungu* would guide them to where they needed to go."

The sun was beginning to set when we finally stopped talking. *Asani* offered me to come to his home to stay a night or two before setting out on my journey to find my father again. He said at his pace, it would take us two or three hours to arrive at the foothills of the Kenya forest that were located several miles from the coastline. He lived in one of the caves with many other homeless people. When I whistled a taxicab down to drive us, the old man could not stop smiling. I don't know if he'd ever ridden in a car before. I suspected he had not….at least not for pleasure. When he mentioned he thought I might be rich, I told him that back in the United States I was homeless, too. After I helped him into the taxicab, he rolled down his window and stuck his head out so the wind rushed against his face. I joined him. We were at his home in fifteen minutes. We would have arrived sooner if it were not for the heavily trafficked narrow streets.

As we made our way on foot into the foothills, I noticed *Asani* moving more steadily on his swollen and scarred bare feet. He said he had traveled this path so many times that he knew exactly where to step to speed up his travel time to his cave. He said he could walk it blindfolded.

When we arrived at *Asani's* sleeping space at a particular cave, he waved me in. There were others already settled in with their sleeping bags, covers, and pillows. Someone had started a small campsite fire just outside of the opening to the cave. There was little conversation amongst the people. One older man was coughing in the background with his head covered up with a blanket. A woman was busy braiding a young girl's hair. A shirtless young man with what looked like tribal tattoos all over his body sat in silence staring out into the night. As we made our way to the very back of the cave, *Asani* pointed out two pictures he had hung on the cave wall of his *baba, mama,* and brothers and sisters. He said it was all he had left of them. He hadn't seen any of his siblings in years. He didn't even know where they ended up when they were all set free by the Master's son. Even though he was the oldest of all of them, he figured they were all dead by now since he was one hundred one years old. They weren't that far behind him in age.

Offering me a rather worn and somewhat stained but clean blanket he pointed to where I was to sleep. I would have told him that I normally used my red shuka cloth as a blanket but I didn't want to offend him.

When the sun was gone and the night took over the skies, I prayed to *Mulungu* to show me the way to my father and to bless those who had helped me on my journey….Auntie *Amne, Dr. Nnamani, Bibi, Jabari, Panya Rafiki,* the Captain and his crew, and now *Asani.* I fell to sleep that night to the chirping of crickets, the croaking of frogs, the song of a bird….or two, and the rustling of the leaves in the trees by a monkey or squirrel. For the first time in my life, I felt a sense of peace as I lay on the ground inside a cave with the only light provided by a campsite fire started by the gathering of a birds nest and the rubbing of two sticks together. I felt a camaraderie with these people who lived off the land and slept in caves….who had no money….who either they themselves spurned or were spurned by the government and modernization of their country….who believed in the God of *their* choice not allowing others to push their beliefs on them….who were somehow happy. Orphans of the world….they and I.

The next morning when I awoke, most of the cave people were gone to start their days by either rummaging through garbage, begging, or performing a talent on a street corner for tourists. *Asani* was gone as well. Probably on his two to three hour trek to the coffee shop where he would sit sipping coffee throughout the day in hope that a passerby might buy him a sandwich and an ice cold drink and, if *they* were lucky, engage him in conversation. At one hundred one years old, there wasn't much more he could do. It occurred to me that the homeless people were not the ones to be pitied….rather it was those racing through life without stopping long enough to feel the wind rushing against their faces or to take the time to listen to the chirping of a cricket or the song of a bird.

Walking out of the cave into the sunlight, I had not the slightest idea where I was headed….*Asani* said *"beyond the forests of Kenya"*….but in which direction? That's when I spotted him….the young shirtless tribal tattooed man I'd seen in the cave. He was standing off in the distance beckoning for me to follow him.

"Praise Mulungu," I thought to myself as I headed in his direction.

71

With each light-footed and quick moving step, the young man covered in tribal tattoos headed deeper into the forest.

"Nifuate! Nifuate!" he shouted over and over again encouraging me to follow him.

I stayed far enough behind him so that if it was a trap, I could escape. Occasionally he looked back at me to make sure I was keeping up with him. I was in good shape but so was he. I would not have been able to boast such an accomplishment if it wasn't for that magical day when at the age of seventeen I visited *Dr. Nnamani* in his dental office for a decayed back molar. I believe that was the day *Mulungu* decided enough was enough....it was time for me to return to my roots. It became more and more evident to me that each person I met on my journey that led me further and further into the forests of Africa was sent by *Mulungu*. Perhaps, it was *Mulungu's* way of paying my grandfather back for his refusal to fall prey to the world of modernization....to remain dedicated to the earth and all life on it....to live off of the land provided to him by *Mulungu*.

Watching the young tribal tattooed man walking barefoot skillfully through the trees and shrubs, I wondered why such a young man was homeless. Had he no parents? No wife? No family? Perhaps he was orphaned like me. But then again, with all the tribal tattoos covering his body, I knew it could not be from a lack of family. With so many markings, each depictive of a story in his life, a Rite of Passage, or a heroic act of bravery, I knew he had to have strong ties to some tribe....somewhere. Tribes do not ban their tribal members....unless one incurs such an infraction against the tribe that they have no choice. All of the older male members of the tribes father their young boys into manhood. I noticed on his back calf there was a fresh tattoo of an elephant. Could this be the elephant walking by my side in my dream? This young man wasn't walking by my side though. He was walking ahead of me....guiding me. He wore only a cowhide loincloth to cover his genitals, otherwise he was naked. On his back he hauled a large rather worn and dirty backpack. I was sure it contained everything needed for his survival.

When we got to the top of a mountain, he stopped. I caught up with him. We had been walking for hours. Night was beginning to take over the day's light. Standing at the top of the mountain, he pointed down to the flat dry land below. A herd of elephants had stopped to rest and drink from a waterhole which with the drought were few and far between. Most assuredly the lack of water was the reason for their migration in search of a wet area.

Gathering up some dry brush, he bent down and began rubbing two sticks together. It was obvious that this was not the first time he had done this as a fire began within a short time. It was my job to keep it burning by fanning it with my hands and periodically adding fresh wood in the way of dry sticks or tree bark. Before walking off into the forest, he raised his hand for me to stay behind. With what looked like a handmade blow gun, I watched as he disappeared into the trees. When he returned about an hour later, he had a large dead monkey hoisted over his shoulder. After skinning it of its fur and cutting the meat into small edible pieces, he began to cook it over the fire by skewering the meat onto a stick. When it was done, he divided the meat equally and placed the pieces on two large leaves, one for him and one for me. Due to the fact that the last time I had eaten was yesterday when I had a sandwich and cold fruit juice at the coffee shop with the old man, *Asani,* I considered the monkey delicacy being served to me as top notch African cuisine. Before we ate, my new friend dropped to his knees and gave praise to *Mulungu* for gifting this monkey a spirit that made him sacrifice his life so that we may survive. I joined him.

While eating, I endeavored to start up a conversation with my new friend. Since he worshipped the God *Mulungu,* I figured he was Waswahili.

"Jino lako ni nani?" I asked him for his name.

"Jino langu ni *Tumbili.*" he replied laughing and pointing at the meal we just ate.

"Ah, *Monkey,*" I said laughing with him.

Then, "Jino langu ni *Chacha!*" I added squeezing my hands into fists and raising my arms to pump my muscles…. *"Strong man."*

Tumbili was a small man. An inch or two shorter than me. Trim and fit with large biceps, a taut abdomen, and muscular legs. Dark skin and hair. The darkness in his eyes is what led me to believe that he could do more harm to a person than expected despite his small stature. This was a man one would not want to make an enemy of.

I learned much about him in the conversation that followed. I was thankful he spoke Kiswahili. He said he woke from a dream a while back at his apartment in Kenya. In the dream, he was running and playing with a herd of elephants when a man wearing a red shuka cloth appeared and thanked him for leading him to where the elephants were. By day, he worked as a tattoo artist in the city. By night, he foraged the forest for food to feed his family. He had a wife and a son. Like most of the people in Kenya, he was Waswahili. He left his tribe when he married because his wife was a modern woman and did not want to live in the forest. Times were hard for them. He yearned to rejoin his Waswahili tribe....to reunite with his *baba* and *mama* and younger brothers and sisters. Before finally falling asleep, he taught me how to prepare myself a bed of leaves to soften the hard ground.

The next morning, *Tumbili* was gone but the herd of elephants were on the move so I hurriedly grabbed up my tribal drum cross-tying it around my waist, tied the red shuka cloth over my shoulder, straightened the necklace of teeth hanging down onto my chest, put my leather sandals on my feet, threw the contents of my backpack into the backpack obviously left for me by *Tumbili* along with his handmade blowgun and three poison darts, clutched the handcrafted *mkuki* wooden spear given to me by *Jabari* in one hand and the coin that *bibi* gave to me in the other hand, then took off running down the hill to the flat land below where one elephant and her calf were waiting patiently....for me?

NINE

As I neared the elephant standing alone with a young playful calf by her side, she raised her trunk to trumpet a sound that mimicked the word "hello"….

"Aaaaaaaaaaaaalo Aaaaaaaaaaaaalo"

When I reached her, she knelt down on her front knees so that I might climb atop her. Once I was sure I was stabilized on her back, she began to walk….slowly at first….then, at a somewhat quicker pace to catch up with the other elephants in the herd. A baby bull elephant picked up the pace by her side. The adult females, called cows, and baby elephants, called calves, made up this herd. The adult males, called bulls, usually traveled alone. I used my red *shuka* cloth to wrap it around my head and face in such a way that the dust from the parched land didn't fly into my nose or mouth. Every so often, if a waterhole was spotted, we stopped. The elephant would kneel down to allow me to take a drink or two from the same waterhole she and her calf were drinking from. By the rising and the setting of the sun, I would be able to determine how long we had been traveling….just as I did by etching each day into the steel wall of the lifeboat. I figured *Mulungu* would let one of us know when it was time for me to disembark my gentle friend's back.

And so it was that my journey into the deepest darkest parts of Africa, and perhaps even beyond, began. I knew this herd of elephants was following a path forged by its ancestors long ago, perhaps as far back as the

Mammoths. I sensed that they knew where they were going and how to get there so I left my life in their hands.

We traveled mostly during the day. The night time was for resting and sleeping. The Matriarch, who is the oldest and wisest elephant in the herd, led the way. She was responsible for making the decisions as to what direction to go, when to stop to forage for food, and when to stop to sleep. Another elephant bringing up the rear kept watch for possible predators or any evidence of poachers. I became quite adept at *catching* my meals. One night I dined on a non-venomous snake. Another night frog legs became my meal of choice. Due to my friend *Tumbili's* instructions on how to start a fire by rubbing two sticks together over a handful of dried brush or a fallen birds nest, I was able to cook my food.

At night, my elephant, who I named *Hediye* which is Waswahili for *Gift,* allowed me to sleep on the ground while she stood. After each night of rest at the first hint of the sun, she would nudge me with her trunk and before long the herd would be moving again. As the elephants moved through the savanna grasslands, they foraged for food often but did not spend long amounts of time in one place. I did my eating when we settled in one place for the night. It was apparent they had an end result in mind and a limited amount of time to do it. It was obvious they knew where they were going. These beautiful creatures weighing several tons and standing up to thirteen feet in height moved gracefully despite their formidable size. Wherein their beauty lie, however, is what drew their most dangerous predator to them....man. Their ivory tusks were sought after by poachers despite the fact that they would have to kill them to fulfill their greed.

On our fourteenth day, when the sun was at its highest in the sky, we stopped to drink from a river in a heavily forested area. The herd took it as an opportunity to bathe and cool off by spraying themselves with the water they sucked up into their trunks. I decided to join them. As I was enjoying the soothing coolness of the water, out of the corner of my eye I saw some movement on shore just beyond the trees. Obviously the Matriarch did, too, as she raised her trunk and let out a loud blaring warning. All of the adult female elephants rushed to land, then pushed their calves into the middle of a circle they had formed around them. I rushed to the river bank, grabbed my *mkuki* spear and blowgun, then in all my nakedness stealthily made my way towards the movement in the trees. When I saw what was causing the tree branches to quiver, I placed a poison dart in my blowgun which was left to me by my friend, *Tumbili,* aimed it at the man's neck who was about to fire a rifle at the adult elephants, and blew into it as hard and accurately as possible. *WOOSH* My poison dart shot through the air and hit its target just as the poacher's bullet hit one of the elephants. The human poacher hit the ground never knowing what hit him. Sadly, so did my elephant friend, *Hediye.* It was then that I felt an insurmountable fury boiling inside of me as I jumped from without the trees and ran waving my spear in the air at the remaining two poachers causing them to run away screaming. Just before they reached their jeep, I flung my spear with such velocity and accuracy that I struck one of them in the leg causing him to fall to the ground. As he did a one sided crawl across the dry brush, I ran up to him, withdrew my spear and plunged it deep into his chest. The third poacher never looked back as he jumped into his jeep and sped off down the road. I was sure he would be back with the authorities to pick up his two friends' dead bodies but I highly doubted he would tell them why they were there since poaching is against the law and carries stiff penalties.

When I returned to the herd, they were all gathered around *Hediye* trying to rouse her with their trunks. After awhile of her laying silent and without movement, the Matriarch wrapped her trunk around *Hediye's* calf and led him away while the others covered her with leaves, mud, and tree bark. It occurred to me that in their minds, they were burying her. I felt that my pain and anguish was as deep as their sorrow so when they finished *burying Hediye,* they raised their trunks and trumpeted a bewailing moan of grief as I joined them sobbing loudly. The sun was setting so we stayed in the area where *Hediye* lay buried. I believe it was to give her calf a chance to grieve as he stood over her partially buried carcass the rest of the night. When morning came, another elephant dropped to her front knees so that I might climb atop her for the remainder of our journey. *Hediye's* calf walked with us by holding onto the tail of the elephant I now rode.

I was soon to find out that my good deed was to not go unrecognized. Elephants are extremely intelligent and capable of complex thinking and emotions. So it was that night as we settled to rest amid the protection of some trees, the Matriarch nudged me with her trunk to a bed of leaves gathered by the other elephants. When I lay down, the adult elephants formed a circle around me as they did to protect their calves earlier that day. I recall never feeling safer that night than I ever had before.

Traveling around fifty miles a day, on our thirty-fifth day we arrived at the Chobe National Park on the northern border of Botswana. It not only was a place of protection for the wild animals against poachers but the Chobe River provided a continuous water supply for them during the otherwise dry seasons elsewhere. As the sun sat half below and half above the horizon, it cast a sultry red glow across the sky. The yellow thorn bush growing into the deep sandy areas swayed elegantly in the evening breeze. Zebras, water buffalos, and giraffes were cautiously making their way from the Chobe River bank to return to the shelter of the Mopane trees. The shrieking chatter of monkeys filled the air as they took flight from one tree branch to another. Off in the deepest clusters of brush, a family of lions lay sleeping. I sensed we were at the end of the road. When my elephant dropped to her front knees, I jumped down with my backpack containing my blowgun and poison darts strapped across my back, my tribal drum cross-tied around my waist, my red *shuka* cloth draped and tied across my shoulder with my cowhide loincloth beneath, my necklace of teeth hanging loosely around my neck, my handcrafted *mkuki* wooden spear held tightly in my left hand, leather sandals on my feet, and bibi's coin grasped tightly in my right hand. Nudging me with her trunk in the direction of the Atlantic Ocean and Namibia which was the next country over from Botswana, the

Matriarch trumpeted to me what I knew was her way of saying goodbye. Tears formed in my eyes but I shook them off because I knew I was closer to finding my father, *Mfalme*. With a stiff upper lip, I took my first step forward and the rest followed easily after that. I wondered if the accumulation of a baby bull elephant would in any way affect my journey as I felt *Hediye's* calf wrap his small trunk around my arm. I named him *Yatima,* which is Waswahili for *Orphan.*

TEN

Having to attend to the needs of *Yatima* now in addition to my own, I decided the best route to take to wherever it was we were going would be to stick to the areas of desert flora, waterholes and, as sparse as they may be, trees. He was small in comparison to the size of an adult elephant so he was easy prey for crocodiles and lions. This was the first time in my life that I had the responsibility of caring for another....other than myself which I had done all of my life. I knew I had to step up to the plate in order that I honor *Yatima's* mother and my friend, *Hediye*.

That night, just as the sun was setting, we crossed over Botswana's border and stepped into the southwestern portion of the Kalahari Desert in the country of Namibia. In this area of the desert it was extremely dry and hot. We walked until the sun was completely gone and we had reached a part of the desert that wasn't like a desert at all in that its landscape consisted of patches of green grassland, thorn shrubs, and strands of Acacia trees. I spotted an area where a cluster of umbrella-shaped trees would provide us with the safe haven we needed so we could rest without being seen. *Yatima* stood over me making sure his trunk was always touching me as I slept. I wondered why he decided to go with me instead of staying with his herd. Perhaps, he was part of whatever plans *Mulungu* had for my journey. I would set out in the early morning hours for....whichever way *Mulungu* directed me to go.

I tossed and turned a good bit all night. It was a restless sleep. I simply did not know how I would ever find my father. To dwell on such a thought for too long of a time would be questioning *Mulungu's* powers so I tried to shove all negative thinking aside. I was in the middle of what I was sure was the Kalahari Desert with little else than the Namib Desert and the Atlantic Ocean to the west of me, South Africa and the Atlantic Ocean to the south, and Mozambique and the Indian Ocean to the east.

The next morning, with the sun beating down on me through the branches and limbs of the Acacia trees that safely hid us through the night, I rose to my feet, stretched my arms in the air, and suddenly noticed....*Yatima* was gone! It was then that I dropped to my knees and began to sob. I hoped that *Yatima* had not been taken from me because of my doubts. I prayed for *Mulungu* to show me the way. Although I had been alone all my life, I never felt more alone than I felt at that moment. I hoped that *Yatima* did not wander off and suffer the same fate as his mother even though his tusks were much smaller and not worth as much due to his age. I felt responsible for him. It was then that I decided I must forestall my journey to find my family so that I might search for *Yatima*. Just at that moment, as I rose myself up from my knees, I felt the ground beneath me begin to quake. Not far off in the distance, I heard a loud trumpeting sound. All at once, through the trees came crashing at full speed ahead....*Yatima!* On his back rode a yellow and brown skinned young man....by my estimation perhaps seventeen or eighteen years old. In his hands, he held a rudimentary bow armed with a sharp tipped arrow pointed at me. Just below the tip of the arrow was a coat of a raspberry colored gel-like substance. I supposed it was dipped in a homemade concoction of venom from a caterpillar, snake, or bee. He spoke with clicking noises which led me to believe he was speaking the Khoisan click language of the San tribe who, refusing to give up their ancient ways, lived their nomadic lives roaming the Kalahari Desert. While sliding himself down off of *Yatima's* back, he smiled widely at me while lowering his bow and arrow to his side. He had a mildly bulging forehead and the absence of ear lobes....both depictive of the San tribal people. He was a few inches taller than me. He was lean and had the body of a young athlete who put out more energy than the amount of food he took in. Black tufts of hair sat atop his head. He wore an animal hide loincloth to cover his genitals and an antelope leather cloak draped around his shoulders and tied at the neck called a *kaross*. He knelt down to draw a big circle in the desert sand. In the circle he drew with his finger a stick person. Pointing at the person in the picture, then pointing at himself with his chest puffed out, he said,

"*Shaka!*"

"Aha!" I responded, "*Great leader!*"

Smiling, I then pointed at myself while pumping my arms and fists up and down,

"*Chacha! Strong man!*"

Then, stepping forward to rest my hand atop my elephant friend's head, I said,

"*Yatima! Orphan.*"

I supposed that he became very amused at the naming of an elephant because it was at that point that he began to roll on the ground laughing.

When he rose to his feet, he was covered from head to toe with the orange hue of the Kalahari Desert sand. His face took on a serious look as he held his hand out at me as though to say "Wait!" then proceeded to draw another picture into the warm fine grains of sand that lay beneath our feet. This time, he drew the sun and the moon. Beneath the sun sat five makeshift huts and several stick people in varying sizes and shapes sitting around a campfire. On the moon side, he sketched a young man carrying a bow and arrow, another wearing a *shuka* cloth, and lastly a small elephant. They formed a line with the young man in the lead. Behind them were footprints in the sand as though they were traveling in the night.

All at once, *Shaka* jumped to his feet motioning for me to follow him. So I grabbed up my red *shuka* cloth, tied it around my waist, then doubled flapped it times two as taught to me by *Bibi*. With my tribal drum cross-tied around my waist, my blowgun and darts supplied to me by *Tumbili* in my backpack, the *mkuki* wooden spear given to me by *Jabari* in my left hand, the leather sandals on my feet from *Bibi*, the necklace of teeth hanging around my neck and down onto my chest gifted to me by *Dr. Nnamani,* and *Bibi's* coin securely clasped in my right hand, we started to walk into the relentless heat of the sun as it shone mercilessly down on whatever life had the misfortune of calling the Kalahari Desert home. Thankfully, *Shaka* carried in the pouch of his *kaross* two ostrich egg shells filled with water. The San were known to squeeze water from plant roots and stems as well as to dig deep into the sand for water.

We continued to walk for what seemed to be miles but because the elders in *Shaka's* tribe taught him the ways of the San hunter-gatherer, he knew the most forgiving and shortest paths to travel. Within a few hours time, we came to a temporary settlement of five huts that were constructed with frames of sticks and thatched with grass and twigs. The makeshift huts formed a ring with a campfire burning in front of each one and a main campfire in the center of all. In each hut lived a single family. Twenty some related men and women were sitting around the main campfire while the children ran playing happily about. One of the elders stood to greet me. Because the yellow brown pigmentation of the San peoples' skin wrinkles prematurely, I was sure he looked much older than what he actually was.

"San Ju/'hoansi," he said using the various dental, alveolar, palatal, and lateral click sounds of the Khoisan language while taking his hand and sweeping it to include everyone sitting at the campfire.

I assumed he was telling me the name of his band of people so I smiled, then nodded my head up and down.

"Waswahili!" I said pointing to myself.

Nodding back at me, he directed his words to the young man, *Shaka*. In an attempt to translate to me what the elder was saying, *Shaka* grabbed a stick from the ground and drew a big circle. Within the circle he drew several stick people with bows and arrows and the

87

footprints of an animal resembling an antelope that they were tracking. After pushing a bow and three arrows into my hands, each of which had been tipped with poison from the juice of beetles, snakes, scorpions, tree gum, or a variety of poisonous plants, he waved his hand at me to follow him and several other of the male members. So I did.

I stayed close behind one of the hunters who apparently was assigned to me while at least ten others spread out in close vicinity of one another. *Shaka* was out front with his father at his side. I was excited. My heart was beating fast. My head was pounding with exhilaration. I felt all of the souls of my ancestors flooding through my body guiding my arms, legs, hands, and feet as my mind dared to imagine my engaging in *the hunt*. This was not a hunt to kill without mercy or reason an animal that shared this land with man. The San are a very spiritual people. In the San's eyes, we were all one and the same. Even though they believe in one god, they also believe that all animals were once human who after a confrontation turned into Eland antelopes. From the Eland, all other animals were born. When an Eland is hunted and killed, it is only when necessary or for special occasions. Through *Shaka's* drawings, I knew that this hunt was special for him. If he successfully tracked, hunted, and killed an Eland antelope, he would become a *man* in the eyes of his tribe. He would then be able to take a wife of his choosing from another band. The girls are considered women and allowable to marry when they start menstruation. Most of them, due to their low fat, low calorie diets, do not start their periods until they reach the age of nineteen. When he picks a woman to be his wife, they will decide to either stay with her band or his. If they do not get along, each simply returns to their band. There is no such thing as divorce drama.

The hunt in the San peoples' eyes is not a competition. When an animal being tracked looms into view and shooting distance, the tribal member closest to it will shoot his arrow. Then, they track the animal for great distances until it finally succumbs to the poison and collapses. They then take the dead animal and cut out only the portion shot with the poison arrow, then share the meat with the entire band.

As we continued to track our prey, only hand signals were used as many animals have sensitive hearing. I was determined to make those putting up with me proud. All at once, *Shaka* raised his hand and stooped down. All the others did the same. Turning to me, *my* man signaled for me to lower my bow and arrow. Not wanting to disappoint, I immediately did as I was told. I watched as *Shaka* quietly raised himself from out of the brush, then ever so quietly pointed his arrow in the direction of an Eland antelope grazing in the distance. *WOOSH* The sound echoed through my ears as his arrow sliced powerfully and at great speed through the air striking its intended target in the side of the neck. At high speed, the antelope took off. With *Shaka* and his father in the lead, we began running through the brush after it. It was a large Eland so it wasn't until three days later that we tracked it to where it lay dead having succumbed to the poison. That night, there would be a celebration in *Shaka* and the Eland's honor.

While the Eland was being prepared by the women to be cooked over the campfire for all to enjoy, the men gathered together around a separate campfire. *Shaka* was positioned sitting on the ground next to his father. It was nighttime. The dark sky was heavily dusted with the stars of the Milky Way. I could not remember ever seeing anything quite as beautiful. One of the elders pointed his finger at me and waved his hand motioning for me to join them. Two of the men scooted over in opposite directions to allow me to fit between them. I sat.

As I looked around this circle of men, I realized how simple yet complex their lives were. No traffic, loud noises, tall buildings, computers, hordes of people rushing here and there. Instead, an intimate gathering of relatives smiling, laughing, and enjoying one another. Everyone's purpose was to see to the comfort, happiness, and survival of one another....as a group....as a people. There was no appointed leader. Decisions were made by the band....men as well as women. The men hunted. The women foraged for fruit and vegetables. There were no arguments or killing of one another. They lived in peace and unity. I never felt so at ease in my life as I relaxed back to listen to *Shaka* tell us of his hunt for the Eland. No one interrupted him to contest his story or to add or deduct from it. They all smiled proudly at him as they pounded the butte of their spears into the ground in agreement to his harrowing tale. His father smiled the widest and pounded the hardest. When they were all done celebrating his successful passing into manhood, the eldest tribal member raised his hand to quiet everyone.

Sitting in the now somewhat cool orange sands of the Kalahari Desert with pyramid-shaped dunes looming in the background amid the stillness of a windless night, I watched as *Shaka's* father withdrew a handmade pipe.

"Dagga," he said lighting it from the campfire, then passing it on to his son.

I knew from the smell that it was marijuana. Although I'd never smoked it before, in the neighborhoods where I lived back in the United States it was not an uncommon smell. Since this was *Shaka's* manhood ritual, he took the first puff, then passed it back to his father who after taking a puff handed it over to the man sitting next to him and so on and so forth. When it made its way around to me, I inhaled it as though I had been smoking it all my life. When the clusters of stars illuminating the black desert sky began to transform into individual constellations and I became acutely aware of all sounds around me, one of the men stood, then sat down beside me. I was surprised by his articulation of the English language as this man, with his face painted in reds and yellows, and wearing an animal hide loincloth to cover his genitals and a *kaross* around his shoulders along with a beaded necklace in an array of colors around his neck and with spear in hand, began to tell me the story of the San people. As he talked and I listened, the *dagga* made its way around the circle again and again and again. As he spoke, another man drew the story in the sand for all to see.

"Many centuries ago, the Dutch invaded our land for farming and ranching. They viewed the San people as animals. They either captured us to serve as slaves or shot us on sight. When the British came, they issued licenses to game hunters to wipe the San people out forcing us to go into hiding. Over time, the San people of the Cape of Good Hope were hunted to extinction until the last of the hunting licenses was issued in Namibia in 1936. Due to governmental pressure, many of the San people have converted to a poverty stricken modern sedentary lifestyle but there are still those who refuse to give up their traditional ways. We have been forced to give up the land our ancestors have lived and hunted on for over 20,000 years. We continue to fight for our land in the courts and recently won a court case against the government contesting our forcible move from the Central Kalahari Game Reserve whose purpose was to allegedly preserve wildlife but in reality was to clear the way for diamond mining. I have been educated in the modern school systems and have obtained a degree in Law. I will fight for my people, their land, and their right to live the way they choose to live for as long as I am alive and breathing."

When he was finished talking, the *dagga* made its way around to me….again….and again….and again. After a satisfying dinner of Eland, fruits, berries, and vegetables, tribal dancing, and divination, I wandered off a bit to lay alone and content in the orange sands beneath the Kalahari Desert night sky with *Yatima* standing by my side as I became one with the universe. In the background, I could hear the San people chanting, talking, laughing, and dancing.

ELEVEN

The next morning, I awoke in the same place where I closed my eyes the night before. The stars and moon were replaced by the magnificent heat and light of the Sun. I could hear the chirping of sociable Weaver birds in the distance as they went about their early morning ritual of building nests in the Camelthorn trees The sand dunes now glowed a rusty orange as they maintained their regal position over the flat land that lay beneath them. A hot breeze wafted its way about the sparse greenery, thorn bush, yellow brush, and Acacia trees that steadied themselves by taking root deep beneath the Kalahari Desert sand. Green round tsamma melons were plentifully scattered about. Their hard white core ready to satisfy one's appetite when cooked and their high water content ready to quench one's thirst. Without any industrial pollution, gasses, or smoke invading the desert environment, I stood to take in a breath of the clean fresh air that surrounded me. The San lived as we were meant to live. Strong yet fragile in that without any immunities built up, I imagined that the entire tribe could be wiped out if they were introduced to something as mundane as the common cold.

As *Yatima* and I walked back to the campsite, despite the sun's light, the fires in front of each hut continued to burn providing protection to the San people from evil spirits. The children were running, laughing, and playing….as all children are meant to do. *Shaka* walked up to me and embraced me. He was now a man and my equal.

He stooped down to draw a picture in the sand of the moon, in a line one behind the other walked a young man carrying a bow and arrow, another man wearing a *shuka* cloth, and a small elephant with their footprints trailing in the sand behind them. The only difference between this picture and the one he first drew for me when we first met was that in the lead in front of the young man with the bow and arrow was now an Eland. He then rose to point to the sky, then himself, me, and finally *Yatima* indicating that we would begin our journey when the night took over the daylight. I had learned not to question why or where. I was in *Mulungu's* hands.

I spent the rest of the day enjoying the San people, their kindness, and relaxed way of living. As the women foraged for fruits, berries, and vegetables, the young teenage boys were off to the side engaged in a game of "who can jump the highest." It was late afternoon when I wandered off a bit to sit beneath the protection of a Camelthorn tree. I closed my eyes so that I might fill myself with the 60,000 years of ancient ancestral sounds that surrounded me….the busy clicking chatter of the San people mixed with the chirping of the Weaver birds, the laughter of the children, and the pounding of the boys' feet as they hit the ground after each jump propelled them higher and higher. I felt free and no longer alone. As my head lightened in weight, my hands began to lightly brush the surface of my drum. Softly at first, then louder. Soon the beating of my drum blended in to a far away yet seemingly close lion's roar along with the soft nicker whuffle of the zebra, the grunt of a warthog, and the jerking spy-like scurrying movements of the meerkat.

As my hands began to play harder and louder to the sounds around me, my pulse pounded, my heart raced to the beat of the drum, and my mind soared to a place high in the sky. I'd heard of out of body experiences before but....

"*AAAAAAAAAAAAAAAA!*"....I screamed as I felt the bone crushing pressure of sharp unrelenting teeth sinking deeper and deeper into my right shoulder.

I dropped my drum and felt myself being dragged like a rag doll across the hot equator-like sands of the Kalahari Desert. The last thing I remember hearing was a loud blaring trumpeting sound along with a *WOOSH* as my limp body was dropped to the ground and I flipped and flopped about to the quaking vibrations of the now red earth. Then, total and absolute darkness. Nothingness. Death.

I don't know how much time had passed as I found myself dipping in and out of consciousness. I first noticed I was laying on a bed of leaves inside one of the makeshift huts of the San people naked with a soft blanket of fur tossed over me from the neck down. Before losing consciousness again, I remember hearing the clapping of hands, women singing, male voices chanting, and the stomping of feet. I felt the coolness of water dripping from somewhere above me landing on various parts of my body. For some reason, I could not move my right arm. Time and time again, I woke to myself howling as an animal in pain might howl. Shortly after, hovering over me would loom into view the blue and yellow painted face of a man with black tufts of hair on his head, yellowed and broken teeth and badly wrinkled skin. The tribal Shaman.

"Dr. Nnamani?" I hallucinated.

Each time, he brought with him a cloud of smoke that would engulf my face forcing me to inhale it deeply into my lungs. Later I would learn that beneath a *kaross* that had been tossed over our heads, he would blow the smoke of *dagga* from his mouth into my nostrils so that I might fill my body with it and allow it to invade my soul and relieve, or at least forget, my pain. In turn, I would then retreat back into the black hole of darkness that I'd come to call *death* where I witnessed the coming and going of spirits that came to me in different animal forms. I prayed for *Mulungu* to show himself to me or to send the spirit of life to wage a battle against the evil deity that had claimed my soul as its possession.

I was told that thirty-one days and nights had passed when I finally fully awoke from my induced coma-like state. When I opened my eyes, a young woman was kneeling by my side tending to my wounds. I remembered seeing her face throughout my battle with death. Beautiful black almond shaped eyes. Long dark eyelashes. Her smooth soft skin a light golden brown. She wore around her neck a healing beaded necklace. She was petite in weight and stature. Perhaps no more than one hundred pounds and five foot one inch....or less. She was very quiet. She never spoke a word. Her face loomed into view whenever I opened my eyes. In her lap, she held cradled in her delicate hands a bowl made of thatch and cow dung. It was filled with water.

"Hui te!" she called out as she ran out of the hut.

The tribal Shaman, with *Shaka* quick on his heels, darted inside the hut. It was then that the San Medicine Man knelt down to chip away at the clay cast that served to imprison my right shoulder and arm. Suddenly, I remembered. It all came flooding back. The lion's roar. The teeth. The pain. Being dragged across the once orange sand turned red. The loud blaring trumpeting. The ground trembling. The *WOOSH.* Then, complete and total darkness.

Shaka, pointing to the soft fur animal hide covering my naked body raised his spear making a thrusting motion with his arm as though he were throwing it through the air. *A lion's roar, excruciating pain, a loud blaring trumpeting sound, the earth shaking, then WOOSH echoed through my mind.* It was then I realized that it was *Yatima* and *Shaka* to whom I owed my life. The animal hide blanket was from that of a lioness….a light golden brown in color with her head still attached and clawed paws swinging lifelessly whenever I moved.

As *Shaka* bent down to etch my near death experience into the parched land that served as the floor to the hut wherein I lay, he drew a man sitting under a Camelthorn tree. He was wearing a *shuka* cloth around his waist. His eyes were closed. He was playing a tribal drum that sat firmly between his legs. Next, with great passion and fury, he drew a lioness sneaking up behind, then attacking the man by sinking her teeth deep into his right shoulder. Then, another picture of the lioness dragging the man out into the sand as easily as a child might whip about a stuffed animal. Next, the heavy earth-moving footsteps of a small elephant charging the lioness with his trunk raised. On his back a young man rode with spear in hand. Jumping off of the elephant's back, the young man thrust his spear into the air striking the lioness in the throat killing her instantly. *WOOSH*

The Shaman, having finished removing my clay cast from my right arm and shoulder, began to chant and dance around me. I heard the clapping of hands and the singing of women's voices along with the shuffling of men's feet outside the open doorway to the hut. The woman with the black almond shaped eyes returned to spoon feed me a broth that had been made out of the throat fat and blood of the lioness. It was meant to rid me of any bad spirits that may have overtaken my body while I was unconscious and in a weakened state that left me unable to physically fight them off.

After she finished feeding me, she bathed me using a very scarce commodity called water. When she began to wash my right arm, I felt nothing. I saw the up and down motion of her hand massaging my skin but I felt nothing. I watched her squeeze water from a root stem and saw it trickling down the deep crusted indentation of a scar that now deformed my once perfect arm but I felt nothing. And then it came to me....*Mulungu* may have taken the feeling in my arm but he gave me so much more....he gave me *maisha*....he gave me *life*....and I smiled as I fell back to sleep.

TWELVE

They say that what doesn't kill you makes you stronger. I am living testament to those words. As a constant reminder of the danger that lurks within the beauty of Africa, *Shaka* bestowed upon me the lioness fur hide. It told a story of a part of my life that changed me, made me stronger, made me more respectful and mindful of life....and death. I decided to spend a year with the San Ju/'hoansi tribe so that I might recover completely and grow stronger in spirit.

So it was that I joined these nomadic people with their strange clicking language as they roamed, hunted, foraged, ate, drank, danced, and worshipped the spirits around them. At night, around the campfire, when they worshipped their god, *Kaggen,* I paid homage to *Mulungu.*

At first, my right arm was carried in a *kaross* fashioned into a sling. I learned to throw a spear with great accuracy and power using only my left arm. When I began to recover from the numbness, pain ensued. To help with the pain each night, the same woman who nursed me through death rubbed on my arm a salve concocted from a pink flowered plant called the Devil's Claw. Within six months time, it regained at least seventy-five percent of its capability. As therapy, I strengthened my right hand by forcing it to join my left hand in pounding a beat on my tribal drum.

Ever since the attack, *Yatima* refused to leave my side for even short periods of time. I believe *Mulungu* provided him with the *mana* of a protective spirit to look over me. The Waswahili tribe believes all people, plants, and animals have varying degrees of *mana,* or power, bestowed upon them to carry out whatever it is that *Mulungu* chooses for them to do. When I retired for the night, *Yatima* positioned himself just outside the open doorway to my hut.

I found myself not needing a calendar anymore as I was able to tell each season by the changes in weather. November through March marked the summer months in the Kalahari Desert. During this time, the temperatures were sweltering hot during the day and night. February to April brought the rainy season. Autumn was a time when the day temperatures were mild and the nights were cool. The flora and fauna were the greenest in April and May. Winter hit in June through August. The days were mild but the nights could drop to below freezing. From September to October, spring was in the air and the days became hotter and the nights warmer. This was a time when the plants began to bloom and new life abounded. One more step toward leaving behind who I was raised to be so that I could fully become who I was born to be.

Upon entering my second summer with the San Ju/'hoansi tribe, one full year had come and gone. It was time for me to leave. Time for me to once again embark on my journey to find my father, *Mfalme.* My right arm was fully healed and functioning at perhaps ninety-five percent capability. I felt strong….and healthy. By stooping down to draw the same picture in the sand *Shaka* drew for me one year ago, he understood that I was telling him it was time for me to go. He shook his head up and down at me. We would leave the following night.

That night, I lay in the hut that had been built especially for me by a people with whom I felt a strong bond. In many ways, they were my family. I looked at *Shaka* as a brother....a man equal to me in every way. I would be forever indebted to the San Shaman who watched over me without sleep night after night, chanting healing songs, and treating me with the ancient medicinal properties of plants, trees, snakes, and insects so that I might heal physically as well as spiritually. I owed the San Ju'/hoansi people, the Shaman, *Shaka,* the almond shaped eyed woman, and *Yatima* my life. I was taught there is no difference between the body, the spirit, and the mind. Without one the other two would die. I would take with me the lessons I learned and apply them to my everyday life.

The next day was spent playing with the children and sitting by the campfire with the elders taking in everything each group had to offer. Even the innocent play of a child provides one with knowledge. In my past life, the elderly were mistreated and not respected for their wisdom. It is the opposite amongst the tribes. The elderly tribal members are the ones who educate the children in their tribal ways and are respected for their knowledge of life and the world around them. Disrespect is not tolerated.

That evening, as the sun began to set and its glow turned the golden horizon red, all the San Ju/'hoansi people gathered around to bid me farewell. The meeting of these people changed me for the better in so many ways....physically I was leaner than I had ever been, mentally I was stronger and wiser, and spiritually I had faced the spirit of death and survived.

My blonde kinky textured hair had grown in length to my shoulders so I tied it back into a ponytail with an antelope leather hide strip. My blue eyes gleamed as they peered from without my dark skin now turned a deep golden brown from the sun. My right arm boasted a battle waged and won in the way of a deep thickly healed scar that glistened when the sun hit it just right. So, dressed in my red *shuka* cloth, cowhide loincloth, and leather sandals, I cross-tied my tribal drum around my waist, hung the necklace of teeth around my neck, clutched the handcrafted *mkuki* wooden spear in my left hand, secured my blowgun and poison darts in my backpack, stuck the bow and arrow into the quiver made for me by the San, then secured it around my shoulder, placed an ostrich egg filled with water in a *kaross* sling made of antelope leather especially for me, and in my right hand I firmly clutched *bibi's* coin. I decided to gift the lioness head and hide to *Shaka*....proof of his status as a Warrior. He was more than pleased. It would be a story he would tell around the campfire for many years to come. As *Shaka, Yatima,* and I walked off into the desert, I kept my ears open attentively so that I might listen to not only the beautiful sounds of the Kalahari Desert at night but the dangerous ones as well.

The following morning, the sun began to once again rise so that it might provide light and warmth to this hemisphere of the earth and all living things on it that had darkened and cooled from its absence in the night. *Shaka* proposed we stay in a mountain cave that had a large enough overhang to accommodate *Yatima's* size. Pointing to the numerous rock paintings on the cavern walls, he then pointed to himself. I assumed he was the artist. I fell asleep watching *Shaka* paint on an empty space on the rock wall with a mixture of red ochre and the fat from the Eland he hunted and killed.

When I awoke, it was dark inside the cave but the sun was at its highest in the sky. On the cave wall, the flickering flames of a small campfire burning at the cave's entrance revealed a beautiful painting telling the story of my life and death ordeal with the lioness. At the very end, a young man with long kinky textured blonde hair tied back in a ponytail was shaking the hand of a half man, half Eland figure. I assumed it was me and *Shaka*. The final frame showed the blonde kinky haired man walking away from the half man, half Eland. Walking beside him was a small elephant and....a woman?

THIRTEEN

Realizing that *Shaka* was gone, I jumped out from under the furred and clawed hide of the lioness that he must have covered me with during my sleep.

"Yatima!" I shouted rubbing the crust from my eyes.

"Aaaaaaaaaaaaaalo," I heard *Yatima* reply with a loud drawn out rumbling noise that sounded like "hello."

"Yatima! Oh *Yatima!"* I happily hollered as I ran to him and threw my arms around his trunk.

Standing beneath the rock formation overhang of the mountain, I stood side by side with my elephant friend looking out at the green flatland expanse of grass that lay spread out before us for miles upon miles. I could smell water and hear the roaring sound it makes as it rushes its way down a steep mountainside to finally land at the bottom of a gorge and settle itself into a pool of water. With some sadness I realized that besides my friend *Shaka* being gone so was the Kalahari Desert….neither to ever be forgotten.

Not having a clue as to where I was, I decided to figure that out later and instead take a bath in the fresh natural spring water that had formed into a nice sized round pool at the bottom of the gorge. As I began to scale down the large rocks that served as a short pathway to the water, *Yatima* swung his trunk at me lightly hitting me in the arm. Grasping my arm with his trunk, he then lowered himself down to his two front knees indicating for me to climb aboard.

He took a trail that led around the base of the mountain then down to a well traveled pathway that led directly to the water. I stood in awe as I watched a few zebras gathered around its perimeter drinking from its depths. The screeching cries of the black faced, grey haired Vervet monkeys echoed as they expertly piloted their way about the trees that sat at the top of the gorge looking down at us. Segregated splints of light made their way down through the trees above to the bottom of the shadowed gorge. I felt as an astronaut might feel when first stepping onto an alien world. Never to forget my near death experience with the lioness, however, I listened even more closely and intently for the presence or absence of any foreboding sounds that may be lurking around me.

When I almost fell off of *Yatima's* back as he heavily dropped himself to his two front knees, I began to laugh at his urgency to reach the water. Having no choice but to jump down, he at the same time took off running. Finding a muddy portion in which to bathe, he sucked the water up into his trunk as he playfully squirt it back out over onto his back. Soon after, I joined him. Tossing my red *shuka* cloth, cowhide loincloth, and leather sandals aside, I jumped into the water wearing nothing but the necklace of teeth given to me by *Dr. Nnamani*. The zebras, obviously having accepted us, continued to sublimely drink the water *Yatima* and I were bathing in.

As the sun began to make its way downward soon to disappear below the horizon, *Yatima* and I headed back to the cave. My only question now was where was I to go next? Up to this point, I'd been guided by the spirits *Mulungu* sent to help me that were hidden in the bodies of others. Perhaps we would spend one more night in the cave.

Just as we came within visual distance of the cave, I saw the campfire at its entrance burning.

"Without being fed more sticks, the campfire surely would have burned out by now," I said to *Yatima.*

All at once, I saw someone or something cross in front of the campfire causing it to disappear from my sight for a mere second or two before returning again.

"Shaka!" I hollered out running as fast as possible to the cave.

As I came up to the cave entrance, back in its hollow depths I heard something or someone shuffling about. If it was *Shaka,* I knew he would have made himself known by now. Perhaps an animal? Perhaps not. Reaching to pick up my *mkuki* wooden spear from where I was sure I had dumped it on the ground with all of my other belongings, I found it to be gone. Dropping my red *shuka* cloth to my waist, then lifting my hands into a fisted position, I prepared for a fight. Glancing at *Shaka's* painting on the cave wall, I remembered my fight with the lioness and how I walked through the valley of death amongst the most demonic of San and Waswahili spirits and survived. Cautiously and with each silent step forward, I prepared to take on my enemy. My eyes, ears, and nose were on high alert. *Yatima* was too large to come charging through the opening of the cave so I was in this alone. I prayed for *Mulungu* to accompany me. One step....Two steps....Three steps....Four....Pause....off to my right, a soft clearing of the throat. Turning, then just as I was about to jump forward to attack the intruder with all the power and might of a Waswahili Warrior, my feet were swept out from under me and over me stood, with *my* spear in hand directly aimed at my throat.......*a woman?!*

She had golden brown light skin. A soft clear complexion. Her dark black hair was long and braided to hang down her back. Full pink lips. Thick long black eyelashes. She wore no top to cover her young taut breasts. An antelope loincloth with an antelope leather front and back flap covered her genitals. She was barefoot. Her face was small and round. Her teeth white. She stood no more than five foot one inch tall. And lastly were her eyes....a deep black in color and *almond shaped.* I remembered those eyes....then it came to me....the San Ju/'hoansi woman who faithfully by night and day sat by my side and tended to my wounds after I was attacked by the lioness!

When she lifted the wooden spear from my throat and laid it on the ground, I rose to my feet....wrapped my arms around her....and kissed her. Never before had such feelings stirred within me over a woman so quickly. She kissed me back. I wondered why she had strayed so far away from her tribe. It suddenly occurred to me that I could not live without her. My heart began racing, my pulse beating harder, a heat starting in my head swept its way down to my feet. Hit by the spirit of love, I knew I would die for this woman if ever need be.

"Zuri," she said softly pointing to herself, then lowering her head.

"Beautiful," I translated her name into English.

Just at that moment, the entire San Ju/'hoansi tribe ran from the outside into the cave clapping their hands, stomping their feet, and singing. In the middle of the cave a campfire was built. *Shaka* and a few other young men came walking in carrying an Eland antelope. The women quickly began preparing a dinner. As they cooked, the fat of the Eland was rendered, then placed into my hands. Following their custom to request *Zuri's* hand in marriage, I presented the fat to her parents. Her father was the lawyer I met on the night of *Shaka's* celebration into manhood. He and his wife gladly accepted it, thus, accepting my marriage proposal to their daughter. The tribal men were busy building a makeshift hut for my bride and me. *Yatima* was outside the cave entrance pacing back and forth while occasionally trying to clumsily peek inside.

By the time everyone was finished eating and the hut was fully constructed, the stars filled the dark night sky and the full moon glowed. As the men sat around the campfire in a circle, talking, laughing, and smoking the *dagga* pipe, the women formed a circle around a separate smaller campfire clapping their hands and singing. That's when *Zuri* and I retired to our *fungate kibanda* or as one would say in English....*honeymoon hut*. Just before we entered the hut hand in hand, I stopped momentarily as the thought occurred to me that *Shaka* might have the magical abilities of a Shaman as I recalled his painting on the cave wall wherein he artistically displayed in its final frame me walking away from him with a small elephant and....*a woman* by my side.

FOURTEEN

The next morning, *Zuri* and I rose from the honeymoon hut that her tribe built for us the night before. Standing guard at the door was *Yatima*. He welcomed me by slapping my arm with his trunk and then raising it to trumpet….

"Aaaaaaaaaaalo."

"Hello to you as well, my friend," I said laughing.

Behind me from out of the hut walked *Zuri*.

"Good morning!" she said softly as she cautiously approached *Yatima*.

At first, he turned his back on her.

"I think he might be jealous." she whispered in my ear.

"Wait a minute!" I responded. "You speak English?"

"I do," she answered. "My father sent me to a school in the city that taught me how to speak, read, and write in English. He said it might come in handy one day. I guess he was right."

"Yes, he was," I responded. "Why didn't you stay living in the city and continue further with your education as your father did? You had access to modernization, computers, cars, machinery, running water and electricity."

"I missed the tribe and our simple way of life. I missed the beauty of Africa….its animals, its people, its beliefs and values. There is too much rivalry and hatred in the modern world. I would rather have my throat cut by the sharp teeth of a tiger knowing that it was done for survival and not malice, greed, or discrimination."

I agreed with *Zuri*. It was one of the reasons I dropped out of the modern world as well. I was happy we would be able to communicate in a way other than drawing and hand signs. I didn't want to tell her but it had crossed my mind last night to try to learn the Khoisan language. I had my doubts though about all the clicking sounds that go with it. I was sure it would not be easy.

Then, looking all about us, we both noticed at the same time that everyone had left. I supposed *Mulungu* had other plans for *Zuri, Yatima*, and me.

Focusing my attention back on *Yatima,* who by this time appeared to be pouting, I walked up to him and introduced *Zuri* to him. When she wrapped her arms around his trunk and snuggled into him kissing him softly on his trunk, I watched as my three year old, two thousand plus pound, hazel eyed, wrinkly grey skinned friend bellowed "Aaaaaaaaaaaaalo," then got down on his two front knees offering us a ride. I could swear he had a goofy smile on his face. I had a feeling I knew where he was taking us as he made his way around the base of the mountain to the well traveled trail leading to the natural pool of water. As *Yatima* played and stomped around in the mud, *Zuri* and I joined him. When we were done, he rinsed us off by spraying us with clear clean spring water.

As we were enjoying the leftovers from the previous night's celebration dinner, I took the time to explain to *Zuri* what my circumstances were and the promise I made to myself to find my father, *Mfalme*. I wanted her to know what she was getting herself into.

"My father explained everything to me and I am excited to join you on your journey," she said. "I love you *Chacha*. You are my soulmate. We are meant to be together. I knew it the first time I looked into your eyes when you were recovering from your wounds. The San Ju/'hoansi Shaman witnessed the love spirit binding our souls together."

I believed her. When the bad spirits were trying to steal my soul, it was her dark almond shaped eyes that led me out of the darkness and into the light.

"EEEEEEEEEEEEEEEEEEEE" a high shrill scream filled the air causing *Zuri* to cover her ears and me to grab my spear. Something was moving in the brush and grass.

Again, *"EEEEEEEEEEEEEEEEE"* This time even louder….and closer.

Yatima seemed unmoved as he continued to graze on the grass and sweet flower buds. Then….SPLAT….onto my right shoulder jumped a….*monkey? Zuri* started laughing. That's right. That's what I said….she started laughing! All at once, from my shoulder that monkey jumped….into *Zuri's* arms!

Holding her hand out to stop me from throwing my spear, she said,

"Stop! This is *Kong*. He has been with me for a very long time. When I was a little girl going to a private school while living in the city, my father took me to see the movie *King Kong*. When I graduated at the age of sixteen, I made

117

the decision to live with my band of relatives roaming the Kalahari Desert. Growing up I always spent my weekends and summers with them. When school was over, it didn't take me long to decide that I wanted to stay with them, to become one of them in heart and spirit as well as blood. One day when foraging for berries with some of the other women, we came across a baby chacma baboon lying next to its dead mother. He wasn't very big. The flys began to swarm around his mother's body and a pack of jackals were circling the area. I took him home with me and nursed him back to life feeding him bottles of milk. Remembering the movie *King Kong,* I named him *Kong.* He follows me everywhere I go. I believe he thinks I'm his mother."

"He's a handsome guy," I laughed aloud, "but I wouldn't ever want to be in a one-on-one fight with him."

Zuri laughed nodding her head in agreement. He certainly was a magnificent creature. Grey thick fur with a bit of black on his face and back and very large, extremely sharp incisors.

"Go on, *Kong.*" *Zuri* encouraged her friend. "Go on now. Say hello to *Chacha.*"

Walking up to me, *Zuri* allowed *Kong* to stretch his face out to within a few inches from mine. A little too close for comfort for me but I trusted *Zuri.* Besides, a Waswahili Warrior is required to show no fear. Suddenly, *Kong* began smelling me, then rubbed his nose against my nose. Before I knew it, a chacma baboon weighing around forty to fifty pounds was perched on my shoulders intently picking through my hair.

"He likes you!" *Zuri* shouted clapping her hands and jumping up and down.

I wish I would have been as happy as she was but I didn't move and allowed him to continue to *groom* me. His weight was becoming too heavy for me so I sat. That's when he jumped off of my shoulders onto the ground and began preening my head, arms, and back. *Zuri* looked happy so I pretended to like it….although I must admit it did feel good to have my scalp massaged in rapid jerking movements. I think he was looking for bugs. I didn't want to know if there were any. After about ten minutes of grooming efforts, I stood, thanked him, and watched as he went to stand next to *Zuri* grabbing her by the hand.

"Hmmm," I said, "Someone else might have a little jealousy going on."

Stooping down to *Kong's* level, *Zuri* smiled. I watched as she *signed* to him to give me a hug. All at once, dragging Zuri with him, he walked up to me and hugged my legs.

"He knows sign language?" I gasped.

"Yes." she answered with a small twisted smile as though it was common knowledge.

Then, *signing* for *Kong* to go play with the other monkeys in the trees, he went merrily on his way leaving the two of us alone.

"What else don't I know about you?" I asked truly interested, "Lay all your cards out on the table so there are no surprises down the road."

I began to wonder if maybe she was too smart for me. Then, I remembered the visit to *Dr. Nnamani.* The visit that started my journey. The powers I was given when the lightning flashed through the window striking my back molar and *Dr. Nnamani's* drill. How I went from being who I was to who I am today. How my whole outlook on life miraculously changed. I realized that *Zuri* had traveled her own path as well. Like me, she had endured trials and tribulations in her life making her who she is today.

"I speak Kiswahili as well as English....and of course, Khoisan." she said all at once and rather quickly.

"Is that it?" I asked smiling.

"Not entirely," she continued with a *get ready for this one* look on her face, "Besides sign language, I have learned to read the intentions of an animal when approaching him by his demeanor and eyes. That was taught to all the children by the elders in my band though."

I stood staring at her for the longest time. Not in disbelief but with admiration. When my head came down from the clouds, I walked up to her and wrapped my arms around her but just as I was about to kiss her, she shouted,

"I am a healer....and I have hunted with my father and the San Ju/'hoansi band of tribal men. I think that's it."

Taking her by the hand, I led her back into the honeymoon hut built for us by her band of people the night before and brought the flap down over the doorway. On the outside of the hut I could hear *Yatima* stomping his feet and the screeching of a chacma baboon named *Kong*.

FIFTEEN

That evening as *Zuri, Yatima, Kong,* and I sat in front of our yet burning campfire admiring the sun's setting and the pink and purple horizon it cast across a waning blue sky, *Kong* jumped atop *Yatima* and began impatiently signaling for us to follow them by waving his arms and making grunting noises. Never one to ignore one of *Mulungu's* spirits, I took it as a sign that it was time to go. Turning to *Zuri,* I was astounded to find she was one step ahead of me as she stood at my side with all of our possessions packed up and ready to go.

Since it was soon to be nighttime and the temperature would be getting cooler, I tied my red *shuka* cloth over my shoulder so that it might drape over my body with my cowhide loincloth beneath. So, with leather sandals on my feet, the necklace of teeth around my neck, my backpack containing my blowgun and poison darts secured around my shoulders, my *mkuki* wooden spear securely grasped in my left hand, my bow and arrows in the quiver made for me by the San Ju/'hoansi tribe slung around my shoulder, my tribal drum cross-tied around my waist, and *Bibi's* coin clutched tightly in my right hand, we set out on our journey to find my father, *Mfalme.* By my side, *Zuri* strode with now an antelope leather full apron that covered her breasts as well as backside which indicated her marital status, healing beads around her neck, a wooden spear holstered to her back along with a quiver in which sat a bow and arrows, a *kaross* worn with one end brought

121

around the back of her neck and the other end brought across her chest then tied together causing it to drape across her front creating a pouch-like sling. In it she carried multiple ostrich egg shells filled with water. A small pouch hanging from her waist was filled with berries.

I could only guess the reason for traveling at night was to outwit the poachers as *Yatima's* tusks were growing and by that alone becoming more valuable. Miraculously, under *Kong's* directions within forty-five days time we made our way out of Namibia to the Western Cape in South Africa on the coastline of the Atlantic Ocean. I wondered if we would be traveling once again by boat. I hoped not because it would not be easy to stow away two people not to mention an elephant and a screeching baboon.

The exhausting trip provided us with some entertainment in that whenever *Kong* wanted *Yatima* to go either right or left instead of straight, he would give a sharp tug on whichever ear was on the side he wanted him to go. Although *Zuri* seemed to enjoy the humor in *Kong's* actions, *Yatima* and I did not. In fact, so irritated had *Yatima* become that one time he shook *Kong* off of his back and threw sand at him whenever he tried to remount him. That, I found to be leg slapping funny. In order that we all get along and play no favorites among the animals, *Zuri* taught *Kong* to merely tap the right or left side of *Yatima's* shoulder to indicate which direction he wanted him to go. In time, *Yatima* allowed *Kong* to return to his high riding position on his back.

During the early morning hours on the first day that we arrived on the western coastline of South Africa, *Kong* led us to a cave not far off from the Atlantic Ocean shoreline where we could catch some sleep. *Zuri* immediately went about starting a campfire at the entrance. Listening to the hypnotic roar of the ocean's waves as they lunged themselves forward to dampen the white sands of the beach only to return within seconds from whence they came, it didn't take me long to nod off into a deep sleep. The last thing I remember seeing before I closed my eyes was *Kong* laying on his side on the ground holding onto *Yatima's* trunk with one hand and sucking his thumb on the other hand as he slept. Since elephants only require two hours sleep per day, I wondered how long *Yatima* would accommodate his new mischievous friend.

When I woke, *Zuri* was already up and about. The smell of cooked meat filled the air and my stomach started to rumble. I had no way of knowing how long I slept other than by the position of the sun in the sky. Probably late afternoon or early evening. More than a few hours left before nightfall. When I walked out through the cave's entrance to stretch, I saw *Yatima* trying to balance himself up on his hind legs while reaching with his trunk to bring a tree branch down to his level so that he might enjoy its tasty leaves. *Kong* was….well, he was off doing whatever it is a chacma baboon does.

Zuri came up behind me sliding her arms gently around my waist. Turning to her, I wrapped my arms around her and kissed her.

"We're having bush pig." she said matter of factly.

"How is it that we came up with a pig for dinner?" I teased knowing full well she must have gone out hunting before I woke up.

"I don't know," she teased back, "He walked into the cave and offered himself up for dinner."

I loved so many things about *Zuri* but her sense of humor was at the top of the long list.

"Where's *Kong*?" I asked.

"Oh, he's out foraging for berries, fruit, and nuts to add to our meal."

I started laughing as though it was one of *Zuri's* jokes but no sooner than I began to laugh, *Kong* came romping into the cave with Zuri's pouch filled with a more than an adequate amount of berries, fruits, and nuts to serve as scrumptious side dishes to the tasty main entree of bush pig.

After filling ourselves with the foods *Mulungu* or according to *Zuri* the San god *Kaggen* provided, we decided to spend one more night at the cave. It was so quiet and peaceful. Unlike where I came from, we were in no hurry. We had no classes to attend, meetings to make, or time cards to punch.

Enjoying what was left of the daylight, we walked down to the shoreline to wade in the cold ebb and flow of the ocean tide. As I gazed out across the wide expanse of water that lay before us, I spotted a cargo ship smoothly slicing its way through the calm waters as though it was a pair of scissors and the ocean was paper. I wondered if I would ever see my friend *Jabari* again, then.... *SPLASH*....I heard *Zuri* laughing as water hit my face.

From then on the fight was on as *Zuri* and I cupped our hands and tossed water at one another.

"The simple things in life," I thought to myself.

After a couple of hours of enjoying the daylight, hand in hand we walked back to the cave. It was almost dusk and the skies were beginning to darken. *Kong* and *Yatima* were waiting at the cave entrance for us. I noticed that *Kong* had packed up all of our gear and had it ready and waiting heaped into a tall pile. He was on top of *Yatima* waiting for us to continue our journey. *Zuri* held her arms out for *Kong* to jump into them telling him in sign language that we were staying an extra night.

"EEEEEEEEEEEE" he screamed shaking his head *no* at *Zuri*.

Yatima in turn started stomping his feet causing the earth to tremble. At the same time, he raised his trunk while trumputing as loudly and as long as he could hold it.

Finally, after a few minutes of non-stop baboon screeching and elephant trumpeting along with the ground quaking to the point of making us unsteady on our feet, we gave up. Just as the sun was about to disappear from the horizon to make way for the moon and the stars, we headed out once again on our journey to find my father, *Mfalme.* Just as we reached the white beach sands of the shoreline, I heard the branches on the trees behind us rustling loudly along with a thunderous swooshing sound coming from the cave. When we looked back, hundreds of chacma baboons were entering the cave to sleep for the night as even more bats were leaving.

Looking over at *Kong,* I nodded my head at him, realizing now why he was in such a hurry to leave.

SIXTEEN

By the time we reached the Eastern Cape of South Africa we had been traveling by night and sleeping by day for fifty-two days. The landscape was diverse in that it boasted a rocky shoreline, mountains, and forests. The temperature of the Indian Ocean waters, in contrast to the icy waters of the Atlantic Ocean, were warm and tropical. We opted to travel through the forested areas to make it easier on *Yatima*. Although baboons don't have the type of tails needed to swing through trees, *Kong* was able to run at a remarkable speed on the ground. Since it was *Kong* we were following to whatever destination he was leading us, we learned at night to count on our ears as well as our eyes when trying to locate him as he often ran ahead of us.

Zuri and I took turns hunting for food each day. While one slept the other hunted. *Zuri* taught me how to cook different meats, fowl, fish, snakes, and insects indigenous to the area. Mopane worms were my favorite. Mostly, we limited our meals to vegetables and fruits. She made for me a gathering pouch like the one she wore so we could forage for different forms of edibles as we traveled. We ate no more than what we needed to survive.

I was thankful when *Kong* finally came to a stop at a narrow river running through a forested area. It was still dark out so after I cleared an area beneath a large tree, *Zuri* built a campfire. Since it wasn't daylight yet, we decided to catch a couple of hours sleep. We all hoped this would prove to be a better place than the last as far as being able to stay a night or two just to relax and take care of hygienic issues. I sat with my back against the tree cradling *Zuri* in my arms while she leaned back into my chest. In front of *Zuri,* sucking his thumb while being held in her arms, was *Kong. Yatima* was standing to the side of us with his trunk resting gently on top of my head with his eyes closed.

I began to dream I was back in New Orleans. I was only eight or nine years old. Walking to school, I put my head down when I passed a group of boys pointing at me and laughing.

"Whack, Whack, Half white, Half black, He's so fat you can see his butt crack." they yelled after me.

Then, it suddenly occurred to me that nobody is better than anybody else! Nobody is perfect. Everybody has flaws. So, I raised my head up and turned to look them in the eyes. One had freckles all over his face, another had big ears, and yet another had teeth missing.

"No Whack, Whack here!" I screamed with my mkuki wooden spear raised above my head and my red shuka cloth tied around my waist then double flapped over

*Waswahili Warrior style. All at once, my shaved bald head started growing kinky textured blonde hair but it was braided real cool like in dreadlocks. Out of nowhere popped Dr. Nnamani wearing his Medicine Man mask, Bibi, Jabari, Panya Rafiki, the old man Asani, Tumbili, Hediye, Yatima, Shaka, the lioness, the Ju/'hoansi band of the San tribe, Zuri, and Kong. They were all standing behind me. Just as I heard a voice say "Hauko peke yako," and I mumbled the words, "You are not alone," I felt........*someone sticking me in the side with something sharp!

"OUCH!" I hollered jumping to my feet.

We were surrounded by a tribe of people who spoke a clicking language similar to *Zuri's.*

"Phakama!" one of them clicked while poking me with the blunt end of his spear.

Still half asleep, *Zuri* jumped to her feet with spear in hand. Then, pulling her spear back to her side, she smiled.

"Get up!" *Zuri* translated to me.

Smiling back at her, I stood. I don't know why we were smiling while in the midst of this apparent threat of danger but we were. It occurred to me that perhaps we both sensed there was no danger. Perhaps these were a peaceful people. The only cannibal tribes in Africa were said to be in the Congo region which was nowhere near where we were now.

Our visitors' faces were painted white. Their bodies colored with the ochre colors of red and orange.

"Xhosa," *Zuri* informed me, "also known as the Red Blanket people. It is customary for them to wear blankets dyed with red ochre."

She then stepped forward to wrap her arms around the apparent leader.

"This is my uncle, *Geffron*. His name means *spiritually calm and having great powers,"* she continued, "He married into the Xhosa tribe and felt obligated to stay with them because the Chief at the time was old and not well. He had no male offspring so when my uncle married his oldest daughter, he asked him to stay with their band of people so that he might take his place one day."

"I should have known," I thought to myself. *"He has the mildly bulging forehead and lack of earlobes that is depictive of the San Ju/'hoansi tribal people."*

As *Geffron* spoke, *Zuri* interpreted his words to me.

"He is offering for us to travel with him a short distance further to where his tribe lives near the Great Kei River in the former Transkei area. He says we can stay with them for as long as we want."

Smiling at him and nodding my head in acceptance, we gathered up our gear and headed out to enjoy his offer of hospitality. It felt good to be awake during the daylight hours.

A few hours later, we arrived at *Geffron's* village set back on a hillside that was within walking distance to the Great Kei River which formed the southwestern border of the former Transkei region to the Eastern Cape. Several colorful round huts made with sticks and mud, thatched roofs, and cow dung spread on the floors formed a semi-circle around a cattle enclosure where they kept their goats and cows. Maize was stored in bottle-shaped pits under the floor of the cattle enclosure. They were plastered and sealed shut with stones to prevent the maize from spoiling. It was eaten when food was in short supply despite its bad odor and sour taste. Although the women still abided by the Xhosa tradition of covering their shoulders and arms and wearing elaborate headbands and headdresses, it was noticeable that the tribe had been affected somewhat by modern Western civilization in that many of the men were wearing pants and shirts. Besides raising their own cattle, mostly cows, goats, sheep and pigs, they also grew their own crops. Still, they live below poverty level due to the long lasting effects of Apartheid that existed in South Africa from May, 1946 until May, 1994. When Nelson Mandela was elected President, he put an end to the separation of color. He became their first black President. Prior to his election, the black populace was segregated from the white and forced to live only in the former areas of Transkei and Ciskei. It was by seeing the Xhosa people living the way they live now that I was able to understand perhaps one of the reasons why my grandfather refused to become a part of the arabic or christian influences and the modernized world.

The Xhosa tribe integrated Christianity into their traditional religious beliefs. As a result, they believe in one Creator but continue to remain deeply rooted in worshipping their ancestral fathers who watch over their everyday lives, crops, and cattle. The elderly are revered as spirits even while living and are given sacrificial offerings in exchange for their blessings. The ancestral fathers speak to their families in dreams but they must be interpreted by a witchdoctor who acts as a medium between the dead and the living. *Geffron* explained that the reason he was in the same area as we were at the same time was because he had a dream where the old Xhosa tribal Chief, who died less than one year ago, came to him. When the witchdoctor was called to interpret the dream, he revealed the path *Geffron* was to take that would lead him to meet up with a man, a woman, an elephant, and a baboon.

The huts the Xhosa lived in were not supplied with running water or electricity so they washed their clothes and bathed in The Great Kei River which was formed by the convergence of the Black Kei River and the White Kei

River at the Lukhanji Local Municipality. From there, it twisted and turned its way for another 140 miles southeast until it merged with the welcoming warm waters of the Indian Ocean.

It occurred to me that in all of Africa's natural beauty, there is another side that goes ignored. Many of its lush green forests have been plowed down. The magnificent animals that once roamed this great expanse freely were now hunted and killed by poachers and trophy hunters for their tusks, hands, feet, or heads. Tribal Chiefs who once were revered amongst their people are now living in poverty. Of all the tribes, the Xhosa have been the ones to continue to cling onto their past beliefs, customs and traditions. They wear their tribal dress during rituals and ceremonies that date back thousands of years. Since dance has always played an important role in their ancestry, that night in honor of *Zuri* and me, the Xhosa men, women, and children dressed in their colorful beaded tribal attire danced the traditional *Umxhentso Dance* to the pounding beat of the tribal drums as the campfire flames swayed and crackled to a night breeze. I sensed the presence of their ancestors smiling and rhythmically clapping their hands as they watched the Xhosa people dancing, laughing, eating, and talking with their heads held high. *Geffron* proudly took his place as their leader. A cow was slaughtered and cooked for our meal. Many of the elders had already

133

gathered to sit around the campfire anxious for the telling of tales of long ago.

As the day grew dark and the stars and moon lit up the sky, we sat around the campfire with satisfied appetites while drinking *Umqombothi*….a beer they made by combining the ingredients of fermented maize meal, crushed corn malt, crushed sorghum malt, water, and vinegar. Since it was the ancestral spirit of the old Chief that led *Geffron* to us, they hoped to be able to call on him again for further directions.

I cannot remember ever having such a good time. My soul was filled with laughter and love. As the night wore on a tale was told of a young sixteen year old orphan Xhosa prophetess by the name of *Nongqawuse* who had a vision in April of 1856 about warriors of old rising up from the reeds surrounding a pool of water. They were purified of witchcraft and told the young girl to tell the Xhosa people they could be purified as well by killing their cattle, destroying all their grain, and not planting any crops. Once this was accomplished, the old warriors would come and drive the white settlers away. Approximately 40,000 Xhosa people died of starvation and the survivors had no choice but to work for the white farmers for food. This, preceded by the Xhosa having been militarily defeated by the British during the Eighth Frontier War that lasted from 1850-1853, diminished their numbers significantly. The colonial governor, Sir George Grey, took advantage of the killing of their cattle and their subsequent starvation by dispersing those who survived to slave labor among the white colonists. In addition, he imprisoned the Xhosa Chiefs claiming they were attempting to incite war against the colony. In the aftermath, more than 600,000 acres of their land were taken away from them for white settlement. Yet, although smaller in numbers, they continue to persevere hanging onto their traditional ancestral customs and beliefs.

Story after story was told. Suddenly, from out of nowhere, one of the woman dancers jumped into the middle of the circle and began to dance and sing. As she plummeted deeper and deeper into a trance, *she sang a song of a journey to the ends of the Earth. On this journey there would be much hardship but just like the Xhosa people, the travelers would survive and become stronger for it.* When her voice changed to that of the old Xhosa Chief who had passed a year ago, she dropped to her knees in front of me and placed a multicolored beaded necklace around my neck.

"Ukulandela le nja!" she shouted in the old Chief's voice.

"Follow the dog!" *Zuri* translated whispering in my ear.

SEVENTEEN

The next morning I woke with a headache. Too much *Umqombothi,* I thought to myself. When I reached over to place my arm around *Zuri,* she was gone. Unsteadily rising to my feet, I arranged my red *shuka* cloth to tie at the shoulder, walked outside of the hut, and stretched my arms high into the sky while forcing a yawn. Off in the distance I saw *Zuri* and *Kong* riding atop *Yatima. Zuri* was laughing and *Kong* was screeching. I could swear *Yatima* was smiling.

"Hey! Wait for me!" I hollered out to them as I went running past the Xhosa huts and out to the open field where they were romping around.

"Mholweni!" each person I ran past clicked to me.

"Hujambo!" I said in return in my native language of Kiswahili nodding my head up and down at them. I hoped my assumption that they were saying "hello" was correct.

Some of the children were sitting in a circle around one of the elders who was instructing them in the customs of the Xhosa. Others were preparing to go to school in the city where classes were taught in the isiXhosa language. When they finished the primary grades, however, English would take its place. The elders looked at formal schooling as the eventual extinction of the Xhosa beliefs, customs, and traditions. Many of the youth considered it a way to bring their people above the poverty level by procuring an education that would lead them to well-paying jobs. All I knew was that I walked and lived the path paved by modern Western civilization for the majority of my life and I preferred the ways of my ancient ancestors. I also realized that what I chose for myself may not be everyone's choice. Everyone must walk their own path to find happiness. What is right for one is not always right for another.

As I ran out into the field to catch up with *Zuri, Kong,* and *Yatima,* I felt a sense of freedom surge throughout my body as everything around me grew more colorful and brighter. The yellow glow of the sun's light, the blue skies, the white clouds, the green grass, shrubs and brush, not to mention the clusters of newly planted green leaved Mangrove trees exhibiting a tangled display of light and dark grey roots above the ground. There was no doubt in my mind that Africa was where I belonged....not the modern day Africa but the Africa that existed before the age of technology....perhaps even before the first word was spoken or before the first fire was lit. Surely before the advent of money, greed, hate, prejudice, government, and politics. I wasn't sure if there was any such place in existence today but I knew that if there was that was where I would find my father, *Mfalme.* That is where I would find my family.

Zuri, Yatima, and I spent the entire day enjoying the beautiful landscape surrounding The Great Kei River, breathing in the warm tropical breezes as they made their way inland from the Indian Ocean, and feeling the warm white sands of the coastline massage the bottoms of our bare feet. *Yatima* was particularly playful today as he swooped the sand up with his trunk, then threw it over his back. Many domestic cows were spread out across the beach either lounging in the sand or wandering about. It was an unusual sight for one who did not live in the former Transkei area. It wasn't long when *Kong,* as usual, ran off for the more forested area, perhaps to reunite with his kind. I was able to tell by the blooming flowers and the thickness of the brush and shrubs, that it was springtime. I could hear the short shrill cry of the Yellow-throated Longclaw bird in the distance.

At the end of the day, *Zuri* and I sat on the shoreline gazing out at the sun as it began its journey to warm and light the other side of the Earth. Fishing boats were headed back to shore with their bounties of fish, crab, and clam.

"Where is *Kong?*" *Zuri* asked. "It is getting late and he always returns before nightfall."

"I don't know," I replied. "The last I saw him, he was headed for the trees"

Standing from a sitting position, she had a worried look on her face.

"I am going to go look for him," she said.

"How will you find him? The forest is so big."

"He always comes to me when I call out his name."

So we headed in the direction of the trees each of us calling out his name.

"Kong! Kong! Kong! Kong!" over and over again we hollered.

Suddenly, from out of nowhere, we were surrounded by several of the Xhosa men. Their faces were painted white and their bodies orange and red. They were wearing strands of colorful beads and beaded tribal wear.

Geffron stepped forward cautioning us to be quiet by placing his finger to his lips. Then, he motioned for us to follow him. Quietly we stepped through the forest. All at once, *Geffron* stopped. That's when we heard it. The swooshing sound made when a body is being dragged through the leaves, dirt, and twigs that lay on the ground along with heavy breathing and panting. Everybody's senses were on high alert. Dusk. Just a hint of light left.

shhhhhhhhhhh clunk shhhhhhhhhhhhh clunk shhhhhhhhhhhhh clunk

"EEEEEEEEEEEEEEEEEEEEEEEEEEEEE!"

"Kong?!" Zuri shouted as she took off running to her right.

Just as fast as she took off running and before I could stop her, she hit the ground. On top of her covered in blood sprang....*Kong!* Clinging to her, he grabbed her by the hand trying to force her to follow him.

"Oh No!" *Zuri* screamed. *"Chacha!* Help! *Kong's* bleeding!"

As we all surrounded *Zuri* and *Kong,* I bent down to *Kong's* level.

"EEEEEEEEEEEE! EEEEEEEEEEE!" he kept screeching over and over again while jumping up and down.

After as thorough an exam one can give a jumping up and down monkey, I could not find any point of injury so I assumed the blood belonged to someone else.

Suddenly, the ground beneath our feet began to quake. The sounds of trees falling and the rustling of branches hitting the ground filled the air. Then, from out of the blue rushing towards us at full speed ahead came....*Yatima!* When he reached us, he immediately dropped to his front knees allowing *Kong* easy access to his back. Drenched in blood that did not appear to be his, he jumped on top of *Yatima* and began to direct him in the way he wanted him to go. Following them on foot, we came to a bed of leaves. *Kong* jumped down from *Yatima's* back and began sweeping the leaves away from where lay buried....another chacma baboon! It was a female. She was obviously pregnant.

"*EEEEEEEEEEEE! EEEEEEEEEEEEE!*" *Kong* screeched over and over again pointing at his friend who lay on the ground before us limp and barely breathing.

Although she was covered in blood, I was able to locate where the bleeding was coming from....the right shoulder area. She'd been shot....by a gun. It was my guess she'd been shot by trophy hunters at the time *Kong* was in the area. He must have dragged her away from the site before they came to collect her remains. *Zuri* hurriedly tore the tanned cowhide string out that served to open and close her foraging pouch that was hanging from her waist, then tied it tightly above the wound on the baboon's upper arm. In the meantime, *Geffron* applied pressure while one of the other Xhosa men located a patch of yellow Aspilia Africana flowers known for their ability to stop bleeding. After pounding its root, *Zuri* withdrew the sap, then rushed it back to the bleeding baboon. When *Geffron* nodded his head, *Zuri* began to apply the sap to the wound. When our on the spot emergency first aid was completed, I grabbed the baboon up in my arms, then following *Geffron* took off running for the Xhosa village.

It was dark by the time we reached the hillside where sat five familiar circular colorfully painted huts with conical thatched roofs. Numerous campfires were ablaze lighting up the night. The cattle were returned to their pens after having spent the day lounging and roaming the beaches. The clicking chatter of men and women and the laughter of children playing grew louder and more distinct as we drew closer and closer. Once having arrived at *Geffron's* hut, I dropped to my knees panting and gasping for air. After laying the baboon on the ground, I threw up. One of the women traditional healers stepped forward beating the tribal drum to match the steps of her feet or vice versa.

"Buya umva," she clicked softly.

"Step back," *Zuri* translated.

I immediately did as she said. Out of her medicine pouch, she withdrew different herbs, then applied those of her choice to the baboon's wound. *Zuri* was off to the side comforting a very shaken *Kong*.

He signed to her that *"a very bad man shot the baboon with a gun. The baboon started rushing through the trees. The man was unable to keep up with her. When she was far enough away from him, she fell from the trees to the ground and no longer moved."*

So upset was he that he began to screech while jumping up and down and pounding his head. *Zuri* gathered him up in her arms and started singing to him a song she'd sung to him since he was a baby. Sucking his thumb, he nestled himself onto her lap eventually calming down.

"Yena ufile! Undizisele imela!" the healer's words rang throughout the village.

"She is dead! Get me a knife!" *Zuri* translated to me while covering *Kong's* eyes so that he would not see what was about to happen.

Blood splattered all about as the healer sliced the baboon's belly open in hopes of delivering a live baby baboon. The gestation period for a baboon is six months. When it was delivered, it lay limp....not breathing. Its legs and arms flopped out at its sides. I jumped forward and began doing CPR....at least what I could remember of it. I learned it along with the rest of the ninth grade in school. At the time, I thought it was stupid. Now, I hoped I remembered enough to save this little one's life.

After a few breaths and pushing on the chest area, the baby baboon began to move. *Kong* who had wrestled himself from *Zuri's* arms was standing over the infant when it first opened its eyes. Catching up with *Kong, Zuri* reached down to take up the baby baboon in her arms. She held it gently while *Kong* peeked at it over her shoulder. It was a boy. *Zuri* named him *King*....as in *King Kong*....for more than obvious reasons.

EIGHTEEN

We stayed with *Geffron* and his Xhosa tribe for a little over a year. So far, *Mulungu* offered up no signs as to what direction I was to go next to find my father, *Mfalme*. *Zuri* and *Kong's* time was centered on raising *King* in the ways of the chacma baboon. *Kong* had taken on a father figure role in his life. *Zuri,* as she once did with *Kong,* fed him, sang to him, and nestled him in her arms to provide him with maternal comfort and security. They both were teaching him to sign. At the age of six months, it was time for *King* to be weaned from the bottle as a mother baboon would wean her young. *Kong* played a vital role in showing him other measures allowed by nature to provide him with the food, nutrients, and hydration required for survival. He often rode on *Kong's* back for their trips through the forest. It didn't take long for *Yatima* to join everybody else in spoiling *King* as he'd allow him a ride or two on his back. He'd become quite a mischievous little imp. In addition to our own little band, the members of the Xhosa tribe were responsible for sneaking him a treat or two when he'd come to visit each of their huts throughout the day.

We were going into the springtime month of September when *Zuri* came to me, grabbed me by the hand, and led me to the banks of The Great Kei River. Waiting for us were *Yatima, Kong,* and *King.* With the wind rustling the leaves on the branches of the trees softly and the rippling sound of water rushing across the rocks in the river, she placed my hand on her stomach.

"I'm pregnant," she said to me while signing to *Kong and King.* "The baby is due in mid-summer, probably at the end of January.

At that moment, I felt the baby kick my hand. As my head began to swoon and my legs became a bit unsteady, *Kong and King* began to screech jumping up and down and clapping their hands while *Yatima,* who most likely was just caught up in the excitement, began to stomp his feet and trumpet "Aaaaaaaaaalo Aaaaaaaaaaalo" over and over again.

Whenever I look back on that moment in my life, my body is overcome with overwhelming feelings of love and responsibility. I remember wondering if my father felt the same when my mother told him of her pregnancy. If so, it suddenly occurred to me how distraught they both must have been at the thought of losing me. So much so that my mother committed suicide at the young age of sixteen because she was forced to hand me over to the foster system.

Yatima lowered himself down to his front knees to allow *Zuri* to climb atop him. When he continued to kneel, I supposed it was for all of us to board him. So, after *Kong and King,* I took my place behind *Zuri.* It was then that I realized how much *Yatima* had grown in height and weight over the past few years. His ivory tusks were at least eight to nine inches in length. I'd read they could grow to as long as six feet. The longest tusks having been recorded at ten feet. He was a massively beautiful, kind, intelligent, and gentle animal. His mother, *Hediye,* would have been so proud.

That night, the Xhosa tribe held a celebration for the new life growing inside *Zuri.* There was dancing, singing, and, of course, *Umqombothi.* The women all gathered around *Zuri* telling their tales of giving birth. According to *Zuri,* they didn't complain about the pain of labor but rather talked about the immense feeling of love they had when their own children were born. They asked the spirits to bless *Zuri* and our upcoming baby with good health, good fortune, and love.

When I woke the next morning, I didn't have a headache since I didn't drink as much *Umqombothi* as I did the last time. I had to keep my wits about me now that I had *Zuri* and our unborn baby to protect. For the first time since I began my journey to find my father, *Mfalme,* I hoped *Mulungu* would allow us to stay with the Xhosa tribe a while longer....at least until our baby was born. I supposed *Zuri* would not fare as well on such a journey as she would if she were not pregnant. Since the path I had yet to travel was unbeknownst to me, I had no idea what the terrain would be like, how much farther we had to go, or what we might run into along the way. *Geffron* suggested they build us a hut for the remaining time we had to spend with them. I readily agreed.

The sunrise appeared even more beautiful the morning following the news the night before that I was going to be a father. The sky looked bluer. The clouds whiter. The grass greener. The chirping of birds more melodic. The warm breezes wafting through the air and swirling about my body warmer and more soothing

As usual, *Yatima* greeted me as I walked out into the warm sunlight. *Zuri* was gone so I figured she was off hunting or foraging for……..

"Wait a minute!" I hollered. "Where is *Zuri?* She shouldn't be out hunting….alone!"

Suddenly, out from the brush and across the field I saw a small woman and two baboons walking towards me. *Kong* was dragging a bucket that spilled water from it whenever he took a step. I ran out to greet them and to assist *Kong* with his apparently heavy load that I was soon to find out was a bucket filled with water and freshly caught fish. *Zuri* was particularly adept at and fond of catching fish with her spear at the shallow parts of the river. Nonetheless, I now had to worry about her slipping and falling while climbing from rock to rock in her bare feet. She had such a big smile on her face though that I thought it might be better to discuss it with her another time. Perhaps at dinner while eating the fish.

If I had learned nothing in my short time in the wild, it was that nothing can be planned or counted on from one moment to the next. When life happens, it doesn't take into account what your plans are for the day. It just happens. And so it was that just as I threw my arms around *Zuri, Kong* dropped the bucket of fish. As the fish lay on the ground flipping and flopping around while attempting to take in big gulps of air, an African Fish Eagle within no more than one second's time swooped down from high in the sky snaring two of the fish in its talons without even touching the ground, then just as quickly heading upward again to enjoy its newly caught meal for the day.

"Afrika tai samaki! African Fish Eagle!" I hollered out to the others.

"Weee-ah, Weee-ah" the raptor's shrill cry warned piercing my ears as it flew off with its prey.

Instinctively covering our heads with our arms, we all ran in different directions to avoid the sharp talons of this magnificent bird. With a wing span of eight feet and a body length of thirty inches, a mostly brown body and black wings, it was awe inspiring to watch in flight. The head, breast, and tail were snow white with the exception of the featherless face which was yellow. The eyes were a dark brown and a hook-shaped beak was yellow with a black tip.

Kong and *King* jumped about the remaining flopping fish clumsily returning them to the now waterless bucket. Thankfully, there would still be enough for a meal this evening. *Zuri* stood off by herself with a sad look on her face.

"What's bothering you *Zuri?*" I asked as I approached her wrapping my arms around her.

"Oh nothing." she replied wiping a tear from her cheek. "I'm fine. Let's get back to our hut so I can cook what's left of the fish."

"Perhaps it's the pregnancy," I thought to myself. *"I heard that pregnant women get moody at times and over things that wouldn't otherwise affect them."*

That evening as the sun began to set and the horizon turned a deep red, *Zuri* and I sat eating the fish in silence while watching *Yatima,* with *Kong* riding on his back, running through the yellow and green brush. It was dinnertime so *King* was making his nightly stops at all the huts in our small village hoping to get a sample of what everyone was eating. As a result, he had developed a little potbelly. I noticed how *Zuri's* belly was getting bigger, too. Before I found out she was pregnant, I thought she had just gained weight. Now it made perfect sense.

Zuri insisted we all get to bed early that night. I noticed her packing up all of our gear and placing it in a neat pile on the floor inside the hut. So as the sun set and the stars took over the sky, we laid down on the ground of our hut while *Kong* and *King* snuggled together off to the side of us. I fell asleep to the rhythm of *Yatima's* slow and easy breathing outside the door to the hut.

Nineteen

The following morning, just before the birds began their morning chorus heralding the rising of the sun, I awoke to the sound of *Zuri* pacing hurriedly about the hut. *Kong* and *King* were still asleep.

"Aaaaaaaaaaaaalo" I heard *Yatima* nervously trumpet as he rotated his position from one foot to the other outside the hut doorway.

"Weee-ah Weee-ah Weee-ah Weee-ah" a shrill cry shot through the air causing me to jump into a battle position.

Startled, *Kong* and *King* all at once opened their eyes while clutching one another as though awakening from the same nightmare.

"Calm down everyone!" *Zuri* demanded, then in a less stern voice said, "It is time to go."

"What do you mean?" I asked.

Taking me by the hand, she led me outside. Perched on *Yatima's* back was an African Fish Eagle. I supposed it was the same one who stole our fish. I then knew that *Mulungu* had sent this glorious bird to assist me in my journey to find my father, *Mfalme*.

Zuri pointed to a recently washed and folded pile of clothing for me to wear. So, after stepping into my cowhide loincloth, I draped and tied at the shoulder my red *shuka* cloth, slipped into my leather sandals, cross-tied my tribal drum around my waist, tossed my backpack containing my blowgun and poison darts around my shoulders, slung the quiver wherein lay my bow and arrows around my shoulder, hung the necklace of teeth around my neck along with the multicolored beaded necklace given to me by the Xhosa woman dancer, snatched up my *mkuki* wooden spear in my left hand, and held tightly in my right hand the gold coin Bibi gave to me so long ago. When we stepped out of the hut, the sun had overtaken the horizon and a bright golden glow permeated the sky. With *King* tucked safely into *Zuri's kaross* and *Kong* holding her hand, the African Fish Eagle took flight from *Yatima's* back soaring high into the sky.

"Weee-ah Weee-ah" she whistled for us to follow her as she spread her massive wings and flew off in an easterly direction.

I didn't know how we would ever keep up with her much less follow her but I was sure *Mulungu* knew. So it was that every so often, we would find our Eagle friend waiting for us to catch up with her while she feasted on a freshly caught fish. We tossed names around as to what name was appropriate for our new found friend. Ultimately, we settled on *Yule nzi,* which means in Kiswahili *"one who flys."*

I was worried about *Zuri* being able to make such a journey in her condition but she assured me that she was fine and would let me know if she could not keep up.

"Pregnancy is not a condition that renders a woman helpless." she said laughing. "In my tribe, it is a state of well-being, good health, and happiness."

I had to admit that this was one area I knew very little about and without any libraries nearby I would have to trust *Zuri*.

As we made our way across the beaches of Port St Johns on the southern coastal border of the Eastern Cape, we stopped to watch a whale and her calf thrust their prodigious torpedo shaped bodies upward from the warm waters of the Indian Ocean as gracefully as a ballerina might execute a cabriole.

"Ah, the wonder of nature." I mumbled aloud.

I wondered to myself how the world would have turned out had man never existed. The animal kingdom seemed to do quite well on its own in balancing out the ecosystem without the interference of man's technology and greed.

It was springtime. From the wild animals on land to the birds in the sky, the fish in the ocean, and the sprouting of colorful flowers and trees everywhere, new life abounded. I was glad we were traveling by day. The temperatures were pleasantly in the 70's which, from my point of view, made traveling by foot easier on *Zuri*. I knew that *Yatima* would not mind carrying her on his back for any amount of distance we had left to travel. The problem was *Zuri*. She would not allow any sort of pampering. She considered herself to be a strong woman and was determined to present herself as such. I did not argue with her. I knew better. I also knew she had the common sense to tell me when she felt she had met her limits.

I soon learned that *Yule nzi* would stop to wait for us to catch up with her every twenty miles or so. It occurred to me that she had a job to do and regardless of how long it took for us to catch up with her, the path *Mulungu* chose for her to lead us down remained the same. Out of boredom perhaps, she often treated us to a fantastic display of aerial maneuvers as we trod slowly along.

One evening, *Yule nzi* led us from the Eastern Cape shoreline to the foothills of the Drakensberg mountain range where I supposed she intended for us to spend the night in the comfort and security of one of its caves As I walked into the nearest cave to determine whether or not we had company, I raised my *mkuki* wooden spear to strike if need be. Slowly, step by step, I made my way through the dark hollow depths of a small portion of The Drakensberg Escarpment carrying a torch of fire I had created by rubbing two sticks together over the dried remains of dead shrub brush and then attaching the flaming material to a long strip of tree bark I had rolled up into a cone shape to serve as the handle. My mind could not help but wander back to *Tumbili*. If it were not for him, I would be walking in the darkness of this cave without light.

"All clear!" my voice echoed out to the others.

Then, just as I took a step forward I realized I may have called out too soon when……..*Crunch!* I stopped dead in my tracks as I brought the torch down towards the ground so that I might see what I stepped on. Whatever it was, it sounded like it had broken into a million small pieces beneath my weight.

"Chacha! Chacha!" I heard *Zuri* calling out to me.

"Over here!" I echoed back at her with a degree of seriousness in my voice.

As *Zuri* came walking up behind me, I was down on my knees trying to put together the broken pieces of the frail dingy white seemingly calcified object that had the misfortune of being in the same place at the same time as the bottom of my leather sandal.

"What are you doing?" *Zuri* asked as she neared my side.

"Trying to figure out what I stepped on. Here! Hold the torch for me so I might get a better look."

Rearranging the small fragile fragmented pieces back together it wasn't long that the mystery was solved. At the same time that I came to the realization that it was the remains of a small human hand, perhaps that of a child, *Zuri* must have drawn the same conclusion as she and the torch dropped to the ground. It wasn't but a few seconds later that *Kong* came running up to us screeching hysterically at the sight of *Zuri* laying on the ground. Thankfully, I learned enough sign language to calm him down. His love for *Zuri* obviously outweighed his fear of fire as he bravely carried the torch to light the way back to the cave's entrance while I followed at a quick pace with her in my arms.

When we reached the entrance, we were met by *King* and *Yatima,* both of whom were in a state of panic. *Yatima* was stomping his feet back and forth in a teetering fashion while *King* was jumping up and down chattering non-stop. Laying *Zuri* gently to the ground, I checked her head and body for any cuts or bleeding. There were none. She was breathing and had a pulse. Feeling helpless, I lay next to her so that I might provide her with some amount of body heat since it was now nighttime and the temperatures had dropped significantly.

"Weee-ah Weee-ah!" the shrill cry of *Yule nzi* rang out above our heads.

When the once sedentary dirt floor of the cave began to rumble and quake, I looked outside only to catch a glimpse of *Yatima* with *Kong* and *King* on his back running across the hilly terrain *away* from the cave. I did not have the slightest idea where they were headed but I had to worry about *Zuri* now. Shaking my head back and forth, I walked back into the cave to start a campfire. Just as the fire burst into flames, *Zuri* began to stir.

"What happened?" she asked while rising to a sitting position and rubbing her head.

"You passed out."

"I remember now! Were those bones you found?"

"Yes," I carefully answered not wanting to frighten her.

"Were they human bones?" she asked shaking her head as if to clear it.

"We will talk about it later." I answered. "After we've eaten."

At that moment from out of the blue, *Zuri* was met with a heavy burst of cold water that drenched her from head to toe. Gasping for air and shaking her head back and forth, she jumped to her feet.

"What was that?" she asked startled.

Her answer stood at the cave entrance where *Yatima* in all his towering height and humongous weight was bending over as much as possible to see if he hit his target.

The tip of his trunk was dripping the remains of the water he sprayed all over *Zuri*. *Kong* and *King* approached *Zuri* carefully as though they were afraid she might fall apart if they so much as touched her hand. When she walked over to *Yatima* to give him a hug of thanks, she held her arms out for *Kong* and *King* to jump into. Standing outside of the entrance to the cave, the four of them trumpeted, screeched, and laughed together.

"Weee-ah Weee-ah" *Yule nzi's* high pitched piercing cry rang out above our heads,

At the same time....*plop plop plop*....three freshly caught fish came plummeting down from the skies striking me in the head. As everyone stood around laughing at my unfortunate circumstance, I could not help but laugh with them.

"Dinner!" *Zuri* and I shouted at the same time.

Because it was dark outside, we decided to stay in the cave for the night but would leave first thing in the morning for the closest town. We owed it to the person who met his or her end in the Drakensberg Mountain cave. A proper burial would allow the spirit of this unfortunate individual to rest and return to its tribal ancestors. I believed we were in KwaZulu Natal territory which was predominantly populated by the Zulu tribe. I prayed for *Mulungu* to forgive me for swaying a bit from the path he intended for me to walk. Then, it occurred to me that perhaps this detour wasn't a detour at all. Maybe it was part of *Mulungu's* plan all along.

TWENTY

The next morning, I awoke to the ear-piercing cries of *Yule nzi*. We slept later than usual. The sun was out in all its magnificent glory. Playfully nudging *Zuri* to open her eyes, she had a smile on her face.

"Time to go." I whispered.

"Um, just a little bit longer." she mumbled stretching her arms upward and yawning.

"Weee-ah Weee-ah" as though on cue *Yule nzi* coerced.

"Okay Okay. I'm getting up." *Zuri* said as she jumped to her feet rubbing her eyes.

While *Zuri* prepared herself for the journey, I stepped into my cowhide loincloth, draped the red *shuka* cloth over my shoulder then down to cover my body, slipped on my leather sandals, placed the necklace of teeth along with the colorful beaded necklace around my neck, flung the backpack containing the blow gun and poison darts around my shoulders, cross-tied my tribal drum around my waist, positioned my quiver wherein lay my bow and arrows around my shoulder, hoisted my *mkuki* wooden spear up from the dirt floor of the cave with my left hand, and clutched *Bibi's* gold coin in my right hand. Lastly, I gently and respectfully placed the human hand skeletal remains inside the foraging pouch I wore around my waist.

It took us half a day to reach a small village near the town of Estcourt in the uThukela District of the

KwaZulu-Natal Province, South Africa. Not knowing exactly where to go, we watched as *Yule nzi* soared down from high in the sky to perch herself on the rooftop of one of the many closely clustered huts made of sheet metal and cardboard scraps. Children were outside kicking a ball around under the watchful eye of an elderly woman. When she saw us approaching, she quickly summoned them to her.

"Phuthuma! Phuthuma!" she shouted waving them inside the hut.

"She's telling the children to hurry." *Zuri* said.

"You know the IsiZulu language, too?" I asked her astonished.

"It is a Bantu click language. It is closely related to that of the Xhosa." she replied matter of factly. "Why don't you and the others stay back here while I approach the hut to try to talk to her. They are apparently afraid of us."

As *Zuri* walked up to the hut and knocked softly on the door, I saw the worried face of the old woman peering out an open window.

"Angikwazi ukukhuluma? Singabangani!" *Zuri* said dropping her *mkuki* wooden spear to the ground then raising her open hands in front of her as a sign of peace. Then, hoping the old woman spoke some form of English, she repeated....

"Can we talk? We are friends!"

Slowly opening the door, the old woman stepped outside barely allowing enough room between herself and the door to step out of the hut. Before slamming the door tightly behind her, she cautioned the children....

160

"Stay inside!"

I was confused. What I read of the Zulu was that they are a very humane, amicable and warm people. They are well known for their practice and belief in *Ubuntu* which means humanness and good disposition.

Zuri and the old woman talked while *Yatima, Kong, King* and I waited a few hundred feet away from the front of the hut. It was hard not to notice the smell emanating from a garbage dump to the left of us where, although there was no activity going on in the village since our arrival, there were a few adult women with their children rummaging through it. In the distance, I could see the towering luxury hotels in the town of Estcourt built to accommodate those who came to sit in a hot tub while relaxing and sipping on a cocktail, enjoying an elegant hot dinner or swimming in a heated olympic-sized pool while remaining completely oblivious to the poverty stricken area that existed no more than half a mile away.

"It is an unfair paradoxical world we live in," I mumbled to myself as I lowered myself to the ground to wrestle around a bit with *King* who was obviously becoming bored.

The sun was beginning to set. The beauty of its pink and blue colours to be enjoyed by those even in the most dismal of places. Just as I worried as to where we were going to camp for the night, *Zuri* waved me over to join her.

The old woman was the children's grandmother. Everyone called her *mama.* The Zulu believe it is disrespectful to call an elderly person by their first name so they are accorded the names of *mama* (mother) for a woman and *baba* (father) for a man. After introductions were made, the three children, two boys and one girl, were allowed to get up from their cowering positions on the floor. They ranged in age from six to ten. They were dressed in, although tattered, clean shirts and shorts. They were wearing improper sized gym shoes with holes in the bottoms.

"Probably were tossed out by children staying in one of those elegant towering hotels across the way," I thought to myself.

Interrupting my thoughts, the children each approached us to politely shake our hands. *Mama* then waved her head in the direction she wanted them to go. Their father worked at one of the bacon processing plants in the town of Estcourt and would be arriving home soon. If they were lucky, he would bring something home for them to eat. Even though they went to bed hungry many a night, we were invited to stay for dinner to share in whatever meager scraps of food he would be able to bring home. That's when *Zuri* jumped up and excused herself leaving me with the old woman and three children.

"No need to worry, *mama,*" I said. "She is probably checking on our elephant and two chacma baboons. They are like family."

By the time I finished explaining how we acquired *Yatima, Kong,* and *King, Zuri* returned hauling three squirrels over her shoulder. She opted to ignore the look I shot her way. We had agreed she would not hunt alone at least until after she delivered the baby. In the meantime,

162

Yule nzi decided to drop four large fish at the doorway to the hut. *Mama* began preparing the food with a big smile on her face repeating over and over again....

"Ngiyabonga! Ngiyabonga! Thank you! Thank you!"

When the children's father came home from work, we were all sitting outside around the cooking fire. Although the sun had all but been swallowed up by the dark of night, *Mulungu* left us a bright array of stars in the sky along with the Milky Way and a half moon. After we were introduced, we sat around laughing and listening to the tales of a prouder, happier time in the history of the Zulu tribe. A time when warriors held their heads high. A time when they wore the bright colors of their tribal garb and performed the rituals and practiced the customs of their people that made them who they were since the beginning of man. A time when they hunted and gathered food from the land that had been in their ancestry for thousands of years. Before eating, *baba* gave thanks to the Zulu god *unKulunkulu* (the greatest of the greatest). Like *Mulungu,* their god did not directly deal with humans. Instead, their lives were guided by ancestral spirits that came to them in the form of sickness, dreams, or snakes. To satisfy these spirits, the Zulu would make them offerings in the way of home-brewed beer or the slaughtering of a cow.

After the children were done eating, *baba* sent them off to the hut to sleep. It was apparent he had more to say.

Once he was sure they were out of hearing distance, he drew himself closer to us and encouraged us to do the

163

same. We waited in silence for *mama* to finish tending to the children. When she returned, *baba* spoke....

"There is much danger surrounding the town of Estcourt. This is why *mama* was hesitant to invite you into our home. She is the children's *ugogo* (grandmother). The mother of my *unkosikazi* (wife). Along with many children and women over a course of time, my *unkosikazi* disappeared. Then, one day a man turned himself into the Estcourt Police stating he was tired of eating human flesh. For proof, in a bag he carried a human hand and leg. Five others have since been arrested for cannibalism. Although there have been no other missing people since their arrest, I fear the worst for my wife. Like many others her remains have not been found and she has been missing since last summer. It has been hardest on the children. They miss their *mama*. Everyone in the surrounding villages are in their homes before nightfall with the doors locked. For us, tonight is a special occasion. We seldom have guests and there is strength in numbers."

When we were done eating, he rose to his feet and invited us into his hut where *mama* had rolled out a mat on the floor for each of us called an *icansi* made from reeds and grass. Two wood headrests served as pillows. The children were sleeping on similar *icansi* on the opposite side of the room. I decided not to cause further upset to this family by showing them the bones of the human hand I found in the Drakensberg Mountain cave. I would make the trip into Estcourt tomorrow and present it to the Police. Just before closing my eyes, I could swear I saw *King* cuddled tightly in the little girl's arms. Outside the closed and

164

locked door I could hear *Yatima's* heavy breathing and the slurping sound *Kong* makes when sucking his thumb.

TWENTY ONE

The following morning after turning over the human hand skeletal remains to the Estcourt Police, I walked out of the Municipal building to meet *Zuri, Yatima, Kong, King,* and *Yule nzi* who were waiting for my return on the outskirts of town. I hoped the Estcourt Police would be able to bring peace of mind to some family by identifying who the hand belonged to. The sky was grey and cloudy. The smell of rain was in the air. A gloomy day….the weather matching the mood of the people living in the villages surrounding Estcourt since the arrest of the five men accused of being involved in a cannibalism ring.

"Weee-ah Weee-ah" a familiar cry filled the air.

I looked up into the sky to see *Yule nzi* soaring downward to perch herself upon the sturdy branch of a tree. When I reached the tree, she took flight again to lead me to the outskirts of town to meet the others. A sudden feeling of sadness swept over me as I drew close to my destination. Something told me this was the last I would see *Yule nzi.* With the others in sight, I waved goodbye to her. Then, I watched her turn around to fly off towards the west with another African Fish Eagle by her side.

"Weee-ah   Weee-ah"   they   squawked simultaneously.

"Now what?" I asked turning to *Zuri.*

Zuri stood smiling at me as though she knew something I didn't know.

"Follow me," she ordered.

167

As we walked in a northeasterly direction she told me of a dream she had last night.

"In the dream I was being led by the spirit of my grandfather. Suddenly, on a ledge behind the rushing waters of a waterfall an African Wild Dog stood in front of me."

"Dog?" I gasped aloud remembering the dancing Xhosa tribal woman who placed the beaded necklace around my neck while saying in the old Chief's voice…. "Ukulandela le nja!"

"Yes," Zuri said with more confidence than I was feeling and as though she read my mind, "Follow the dog!"

Perhaps this was another spirit sent by *Mulungu to* guide me. Never one to ignore any of *Mulungu's* signs, I followed *Zuri* knowing that no matter what danger might present itself on my journey, the goal to find my father, *Mfalme,* would remain unchanged. As we walked beneath the grey clouds, they shouted their anger at us with loud claps of thunder and the drizzling of rain. I wondered what I might have done to displease *Mulungu.* Then, in remembering back on how much joy rain brought to our tribal friends all along the Kalahari Desert, I realized that perhaps a bit of my thinking remained Westernized wherein water was plentiful and rain didn't need to be accumulated in an ostrich shell, by digging a deep hole, or by stroking the roots of a plant in order that one might quench his thirst.

Nonetheless, the rain continued throughout the day. Finally, just as the grey day skies began to darken to night….just as in *Zuri's* dream….we settled ourselves on a ledge that sat nestled from sight behind one of the many waterfalls decorating the massive landscape of The Great Escarpment. I started a campfire while *Zuri* prepared a meal of fruits and insects. In front of us, she laid four ostrich shells filled with water from the rain. That night I decided an apology to *Mulungu* was in order.

Snuggled together, *Zuri* and I warmed ourselves by the campfire while *Yatima* took refuge on the ground level below a mountain overhang. *Kong* and *King* stayed with *Yatima* huddled together beneath the safety of his large stature.

Zuri's stomach was noticeably bigger. When I began to play my Waswahili tribal drum, *Zuri* said she felt our baby kicking to the beat.

"What a beautiful night," I thought to myself as my hands were taken over by the spirits of my Waswahili ancestors.

I felt myself transcending to a state of consciousness beyond that of this earth. Higher….higher….higher. Suddenly, in and out of the stars in the sky, I watched as *Zuri* joined me, her body swaying and dancing to the beat of my tribal drum as its music filled the skies. It wasn't long when I realized we were dancing amongst the constellations in the galaxy Canis Majoris. With *Zuri* leading the way, her feet rhythmically tapped a path to the star Syrius. It occurred to me that another name for Syrius was The Dog Star. Settling myself next to *Zuri* as we twirled and danced our way around the bright blue light of Syrius, I felt the multi-colored necklace bequeathed to me by the dancing Xhosa Tribal woman swaying to the

169

beat back and forth across my chest and heard her words in the old Chief's voice echo throughout the universe...."Ukulandela le nja!"

The next thing I knew, I was back on the ledge that sat hidden behind the rushing white waters of the waterfall. My hands continued to play the tribal drum until *Zuri* came to rest herself beside me. Laying the drum aside, I placed my red shuka cloth over *Zuri,* then crawled in next to her. We both fell asleep smiling.

TWENTY TWO

The next morning, I awoke to a deep low growling sound in my right ear. I dared not open my eyes or move a muscle. I hoped if *Zuri* heard it, she would not move as well. The sound it was making indicated that it had to be a wolf, a jackal, a hyena, or….an African Wild Dog. Based on *Zuri's* dream, I decided on the latter. As I lay struggling in my mind to come up with a plan to subdue or even kill this animal that posed a threat to not only me but *Zuri* and our unborn baby, *Zuri* suddenly jumped up from beneath my red *shuka* cloth with spear raised high in the air. Just as she lunged at the "dog," he quickly jumped back, layed down, and began to whine.

"Get up, *Chacha!*" she hollered at me.

I rose in complete embarrassment for not having done what she did before she did it so I attempted to feign being aware of it at all. When *Zuri* began to take a step forward to approach the dog, I grabbed her by the arm to hold her back. After all, I had to demonstrate some degree of masculinity. I then stepped cautiously and carefully forward. When I reached the dog, it rolled over on its back encouraging a belly rub.

It was an African Wild Dog. With a quick on the spot estimation, I guessed it to be perhaps twenty-five to thirty inches to its shoulders in height and around fifty to sixty pounds in weight. It wore a colorful patchy fur coat that was irregularly blotched with shades of brown, black, beige and white. Long limbed. Four toes on each foot.

Broad flat head. Short muzzle. Large erect bowl-shaped ears. Long tasseled tail. Sounds ranging from shrill chirping to deep short grunting puffs of air. Sharp incisors. It was the latter that made me even more cautious in accepting its act of playfulness as a sign of friendship. However, after having failed to be the first to display any form of dominance over this wild creature, I puffed my chest out and bravely approached it by kneeling down and rubbing its belly. Thankfully, it continued to wriggle about on its back enjoying the massaging movements of my hands. When I stood, it did too....this time, wagging its tail

Zuri then leaned over to pet our new canine friend on the head. Although the African Wild Dog was a social animal, its socialism was restricted only to the fourteen to sixteen other dogs in its pack. It had never been known to be domesticated to the point of living with man. Since this way of behaving was not typical of this species, I had to believe he was sent from *Mulungu* to lead me further on my journey to find my father, *Mfalme*. We decided to name him *Mbwa* which in Kiswahili means *"dog."*

As *Kong* and *King* came rushing over to us, I could hear *Yatima* shifting his weight from one side to the other while nervously trumpeting repeatedly....

"Aaaaaaaaaaaloo! Aaaaaaaaaaalo!"

"I'm sorry," I shouted, "Where are my manners? *Kong* and *King*, I would like you to meet *Mbwa*. He will be leading me further on my journey to find my father."

Kong held his hand out to push *King* back while he stepped cautiously forward. *King* jumped into *Zuri's* arms. When *Kong* bravely brought his face to within an inch or

172

two away from *Mbwa's* nose. they both stood staring at one another as though frozen….as if there was a line drawn and neither wanted to step over it. When *Kong* began to sniff unsuredly, so did *Mbwa*. Their eyes remained transfixed one upon the other's. *Kong* made the first move by raising both arms and placing them around *Mbwa's* neck. *Mbwa* reciprocated by licking *Kong's* face. Then, to break the ice I suppose, ever adventurous *King* jumped down from *Zuri's* arms landing between them. After that, they jumped and played about as though they had known one another forever.

"Aaaaaaaaaaalo! Aaaaaaaaaaaalo!" *Yatima* bellowed pitifully.

Running outside to *Yatima's* side, I called out to *Mbwa*. He immediately ran to me while I stroked *Yatima's* trunk to calm him. *Yatima* remained cautious in his introduction to *Mbwa* but became more accepting as he watched *Kong* and *King* romping about with him.

After enjoying a breakfast of foraged blackberries, cherries, and plums, I stood to don my red *shuka* cloth, cowhide loincloth, necklace of teeth, necklace of multi-colored beads, and leather sandals. Following that, I proceeded to cross-tie my tribal drum around my waist along with my foraging pouch, hoist my quiver of bow and arrows around my shoulder, and stabilize my backpack across my back which among other necessities contained my blowgun and darts. Then, after seeing that *Zuri* was already patiently waiting for me with *Mbwa* by her side, I grabbed up my *mkuki* spear in my left hand, and held

173

tightly in my right hand the coin given to me by *Bibi*. Taking in a deep breath, I looked at Mbwa then said....

"Okay, *Mbwa!* Let's go!"

With that, *Mbwa* barked what sounded like a squeaky sneeze, then took off in a northeastern direction saying goodbye to the province of Kwazulu-Natal that lay in the southeast portion of the country of South Africa in the second largest continent of the world....Africa.

TWENTY THREE

And so it was, we walked for miles and days on end. At night, we ate and slept. During the day, we walked....and walked....and walked. *Zuri's* stomach had grown to such proportions that I thought her skin could stretch no more. I was sure I would awaken one morning to find her laying with her stomach split open and a baby lying between us. Such a thought horrified me to the extent that I willed myself not to think it anymore.

We were well into summer now and I knew our baby was due to arrive soon. *Zuri* was in full nesting mode as she spent much of the early evening hours preparing for the baby. For traveling, she intended to carry our newborn in her *kaross* that fit across her chest as a large sling. This would allow the baby easy access to the breast. A back wrap carry-cross made of a rectangular shaped strong, soft material and the bright red and orange colors given to her by the women of the San Ju'hoansi tribe would be used instead of the *kaross* when he, or she, grew bigger and older. Using *King* as a "prop" she demonstrated to me how it was to be worn. Bending over, she had me place *King* facing forward on her back. After placing the center of the wrap on his back, she brought one wrap end over her shoulder and the other wrap end under the opposite arm where the two ends met at her mid-chest area and were securely tied together creating a back wrap seat for the child to ride safely and comfortably in.

Mbwa, Yatima, Kong, and King had become good friends over our months of traveling. I often wondered if *Mbwa* would stay with us when we reached our next destination or if he would return to his pack. Perhaps, we were his pack now. He was a fierce hunter. He often disappeared in the early morning or late evening hours only to return dragging a portion of his kill to share with us. For whatever reason, when it was time to sleep, he curled up next to me. I hoped not because he thought of me as the weakest in need of protection but rather that I was the leader of this mismatched part human, part animal tribe. A Chief of sorts I imagine

During the day, we enjoyed the warm white sand beaches beneath our feet, the tropical turquoise waters of the Indian Ocean spread out across the horizon as far as the eye could see, and the blue skies above our heads as we walked along the coastline of the country of Mozambique in the southeast of Africa. Each night before nightfall, we headed inland to seek refuge amongst a flatland of green, yellow, red, and brown trees, flowers, and brush. It was not uncommon to pass by herds of elephants, zebras, and giraffes drinking leisurely together at a watering hole as the sun began to disappear below the red and golden skies of the horizon. If we were quiet, they ignored us. Beyond the flatland lay mountainous terrain that ranged from the lowest elevations of Serra Nhatoa and Mepulo at 6070 feet to the highest of Mount Binga at 7992 feet.

I noticed a bit of a tug of war going on between *Zuri* and *Mbwa* at a point in Mozambique where *Zuri* wanted to turn inland from the coastline of the Indian Ocean and

Mbwa wanted to go deeper into Mozambique. It appeared that *Zuri* won the battle as *Mbwa* eventually gave in to her wishes and allowed her to take the lead. I learned long ago to remain silent and allow *Mulungu* to lead me in whatever direction he chose for me which I assumed included or at least allowed for a step or two off the beaten path. Changing course, we began backtracking inland until we reached the province of Limpopo. Situated in the northeastern corner of South Africa, it is often called the Gateway to Africa because it shares its border with the three neighboring countries of Botswana, Zimbabwe, and Mozambique.

When *Zuri* picked a spot to rest beneath a very large baobab tree, I hoped we would be spending the night. I noticed her breathing had gone from soft and easy to short and laborious over the last several hours. I figured it was because of the extra weight she was carrying around not to mention the tremendous amount of swelling that had settled in her face, feet, legs, and hands. She never complained. She insisted on pulling her half of the load on our journey which included hunting, foraging, cooking as well as watching over *Yatima, Kong, King, Mbwa*....and me. Every night, in addition to thanking *Mulungu* for providing the *mana* necessary to *Auntie Amne, Dr. Nnamani, Bibi, Jabari, Panya Rafiki, Asani, Tumbili, Hediye, Yatima, Shaka, Geffron, Kong, King, Yule nzi, and Mbwa* to guide me on my journey to find my father, *Mfalme,* I thanked him for the love of my life....*Zuri.* She was a strong, loving, giving woman. She gave me a reason to live. She was instrumental in helping me make the transformation from who I was forced to be to who I was born to be. I could not imagine life without her.

The baobab tree she selected for us to rest beneath was at least ninety feet tall and fifty some feet around. The uniqueness of this particular type of tree is that its huge trunk is hollowed out and able to provide safety and security to as many as one-hundred people at a time. It is called the *Tree of Life*. When *Yatima* saw the string of baobab trees, he ran to one nearby so he could eat its cork-like bark. Due to its branches of leaves being so small that they could be mistaken for the tree's roots in comparison to its extremely large round trunk, the story was that the Gods became so angry at its appearance that they threw it to the Earth where it landed upside down.

When I went to take a step inside the trunk, *Zuri* stopped me shaking her head *no* at me. I stopped. I remembered her explaining to me that like many other African tribal women when it was time to give birth, a San Ju/'hoansi woman would wander off from the rest of the tribe, dig a hole in the ground, line it with leaves, and deliver her baby alone.

Before disappearing into the darkness of the hollow trunk, *Zuri* handed me her foraging pouch. Not knowing what else to do with myself, I began to build a campfire on the dry land surrounding the tree. *Yatima* came rushing over to block the tree's entrance just as *Mbwa* positioned himself in front of me so that I could see his dark glaring eyes. When I turned to look in the direction of the baobab tree, *Mbwa* dug his front paw nails into the ground, lowered his head, and snarled a low threatening growl warning me to stay put. *Kong* and *King* busied themselves by climbing a neighboring baobab tree. When they returned they brought with them three of the tree's egg-shaped woody shelled fruits that when opened revealed dark colored kernels and a tangy powder. After cracking one open for me, they kept the other two for themselves. Adding some water to the fruit from one of *Zuri's* water filled ostrich eggs, I decided to mix its contents with the insects and plants in *Zuri's* foraging pouch. To my surprise, it resulted in a tasty meal with a citrusy sweet flavor. I saved half for *Zuri*.

I listened intently for any sounds coming from the hollow of the tree as the daylight was swallowed up by the night. *Yatima* continued to stand strong at his post guarding the tree's entrance. Climbing atop his back *Kong* and *King* joined him by serving as lookouts. I began to pace back and forth. *Mbwa* joined me.

All at once breaking the silence of night, a baby's cry loudly echoed over and over again from out of the hollow trunk announcing to the world its arrival. I stood frozen in time….waiting to hear *Zuri's* voice calling me to join her. My heart was beating so fast and hard I thought I might fall unconscious to the ground. Not wanting to disappoint *Zuri*, I forced myself to slow my breathing by taking deep breaths in and then out, in and then out, in and then out. Once settled and calmed enough to think straight, I remembered *Zuri* telling me that after the baby was born, she wouldn't make an appearance right away since time was needed for the placental cord to stop pulsating before cutting it.

Some time later, *Zuri* stepped outside of the hollowed tree. She was naked and holding the baby to her breast. Yatima kneeled so that she could easily climb atop him. No words were spoken but when he started walking, I followed behind on foot. *Kong, King,* and *Mbwa* trailed closely behind. Stopping at the bank of a narrow river, Yatima knelt again to allow *Zuri* to lower herself and the baby to the ground. Once *Zuri* was knee deep in the water, she bent to wash the baby, then gently handed it over from her arms to mine. It was then that I saw we had a son. Holding the baby as high in the air as possible I hollered in my loudest deepest voice….

"Mtu huyo aitwaye….*SAFARI!*"

And then again in an even louder deeper voice, this time with tears streaming down my face….

"He shall be named….*SAFARI!*"

TWENTY FOUR

Two years passed since *Safari's* birth. It is Waswahili tradition to name one's first born after one of their parents or grandparents. Although the name I chose was not mine nor that of my father, *Mfalme,* it described our situation at the time of his birth. *Safari* means *"born while traveling....a journey."* Besides, there was a very small part of me that thought my father might reject me....or would not believe me....or was not the father I dreamed him to be....if I found him, that is.

Safari was a happy child. He always had a smile on his face. He was a handsome boy. Unique. He had his mother's soft golden brown skin color and almond shaped eyes. Although his hair was black in color like his mother's, its texture was smooth and straight....I imagine like my mother Sarah's. His eyes were as blue as the sky on a warm summer day....like mine. He was a living symbol of my love for *Zuri* and hers for me. *Kong, King, Yatima,* and *Mbwa* kept an ever watchful eye on him. At night, while he slept coddled in his mother's arms, they formed a protective sleeping circle around him. Since *Yatima* was too big to enter the hollowed out baobab tree trunk that had become our home in the province of Limpopo, he stood guard at its opening.

At the time, for whatever reason, *Mulungu* must have had other plans for me. Perhaps, he decided to wait a while before continuing my journey to find my father in order that *Safari* could grow so that he would be better able to endure such an undertaking. We had become quite comfortable in our new home. *Zuri* looked and felt stronger than ever before. Ever since *Safari* took his first step, he and I ventured out each early morning to hunt. In the beginning, he rode on my shoulders serving as lookout for whatever prey we might encounter. I often relied on the dreams I had of myself and my own father, *Mfalme*, running through the forests together as he taught me his skills in hunting. Just as *Zuri* taught me, she also taught our son how to forage for *edible* and *safe* plants, vegetables, insects, and fruits.

African tribal women breastfeed their children until the age of three years so when *Safari* reached the age of four, *Zuri* gave birth to another child....this time a girl. She named her *Nobomi*. It means *Life* in the isiXhosa language. She was as beautiful as *Safari* was handsome. She was born with blonde kinky textured hair, blue almond shaped eyes, full lips, and soft golden brown skin. A quiet child. A dreamer. A thinker. She adored her brother and he was very protective of her.

By the time *Safari* turned five, he was proficient in both hunting and foraging. *Mbwa* taught him how to swim....dog paddle, that is. *Kong* and *King* taught him how to climb the tallest of trees with agility and ease. *Yatima* never tired of riding him around atop his back in play. He learned how to bark like a dog, screech like a baboon, trumpet like an elephant, and talk like a human. Under *Zuri's* guidance, he was able to speak many of the African tribal languages in addition to English. Since Zuri received her education in the city through formal schooling, she taught him how to read, write, and mathematize. His education far surpassed that of any he would have gotten in a formal school. I made sure he and I were as close as any father and son could ever be. Our bond was tight. I wanted my son to have everything I did not have growing up in terms of love, family, and confidence.

At bedtime, *Safari* climbed onto my lap as *Zuri* took a place by the campfire breastfeeding and coddling *Nobomi* while I told them the story of *Sarah* and *Mfalme* and how I came to be. It was important to me that both *Safari* and *Nobomi* understand that my journey was just as important to them as it was to me. It was a part of our ancestry. Our heritage. It was a hole within us that needed to be filled. The day would come when they would meet their mother's tribal family. We had yet to find mine.

In the meantime, *Zuri* taught *Safari* and *Nobomi* the customs of the San Ju'hoansi tribe while I taught them the ways of the Waswahili. Most importantly, we made sure they knew our story….all of the hows, whens, wheres, and whys we met and fell in love.

Safari often played with neighboring children from the Venda tribe. They lived in conical thatch roofed houses near the enchanted Lake Fundudzi. Lake Fundudzi is their sacred body of water surrounded by the mythical Thathe Vondo Forest high in the Soutpansberg Mountains in Limpopo. Old women with sticks on their heads were said to appear out of the mist and then disappear in a burst of green. The forest, where many spirits reside, is protected by two spirits known as *Nethane* and *Ndadzi*. *Nethane* is half man, half lion and *Ndadzi* is a lightning bird.

Lake Fundudzi is protected by the Great White Python and is infested with crocodiles. So that they may be blessed with rain the following season and a good harvest, the Venda girls perform the *Domba* dance annually to honor the Python. They line up facing forward one behind the other and move their interconnected arms in a slithering snake-like movement. Strangers are not allowed near the Lake. If a stranger does receive permission from the Venda Chief to near its shores, he must first stand with his back facing it, then bend so that he looks at it with his head upside down between his legs.

I taught *Safari* the practice of *Animism*. Each night we gave thanks to the god *Mulungu* and those he chose to fill with the power of *mana* so that they could direct me on my journey to find my father, *Mfalme*. I told him how *Auntie Amne, Dr. Nnamani, Bibi, Jabari, Panya Rafiki, Asani, Tumbili, Hediye, Yatima, Zuri, Kong, King, Shaka, Geffron, Yule nzi, and Mbwa* all played a part in bringing me to where I was now.

Then one night, just as I was thinking that so much time had passed that perhaps this was where *Mulungu* intended me to be, we received an invitation to join in the ceremonies of the Venda tribe. Since polygamy is common amongst them, their Chief was going to select a new bride this night from one of the girls dancing the Domba. The annual dance not only paid homage to the Great White Python but signified the girls' final rite of passage into womanhood as well.

Zuri and I were excited. For *Zuri,* this meant other women to converse with and maybe to even forage with.

For me, it was an opportunity to learn another tribe's customs. When I thought *Mulungu* might introduce to me the next person or animal he selected to lead me further on my journey, my heart began to beat faster. I was also excited about meeting new people....to laugh, talk, and perhaps smoke a little *dagga.* I had changed from my younger days back in the States. I no longer avoided others to escape being ridiculed. *"Whack"* no longer existed. The man who existed today would not allow such cruelty and bullying. Today they might meet the tip of my *mkuki* spear.

Safari and *Nobomi* were joining us this night. *Safari* loved playing with the Venda children and *Nobomi,* now one years old, was just learning to walk. The older girls would enjoy caring for and playing with her. *Yatima, Kong, King,* and *Mbwa,* however, were asked to stay behind. We did not know how the Venda tribe would react if we brought our animal friends with us. Besides, it would be impolite to add any more to our party than were invited.

After bathing in the Limpopo river, I donned my freshly washed red *shuka* cloth and tied it at the shoulder so it draped down to cover my body, stepped into my cowhide loincloth and leather sandals, and placed the necklace of teeth and colorful beaded necklace around my neck. *Zuri* then tightly braided my long kinky textured blonde hair.

When *Zuri* finished readying herself, I grabbed hold of my son's hand. *Nobomi* climbed onto *Zuri's* back and sat comfortably sucking her thumb in the bright red and orange back wrap carry-cross.

Meeting up with the Chief of the Venda tribe, he led us to Lake Fundudzi warning us not to look at the lake until

185

we first stood with our backs to it and bent over to view it with our heads between our legs. After having followed his instructions, we were able to join the other members of the Venda tribe. I was led to where the men were gathered sitting around a campfire laughing and talking. *Zuri* joined the women who were busy cooking that evening's meal. *Nobomi* was swept up by a group of giggling teenage girls and *Safari* ran off to play with the other children.

While sitting by the fire with the men, I soon realized that their language being a Bantu language as is Kiswahili, I was able to understand a good deal of what they were saying without an interpreter. The Venda are a spiritual people. As evening neared, the girls picked to dance the Domba postured themselves in a line, one behind the other, hands and arms interconnected. With the campfires burning and the sun set, the girls lined up at the lake to begin dancing the Domba to the beat of one thungwa, one ngoma and three murumba drums. In unity they slithered like a snake and stepped forward in a clockwise direction as they danced to appease the Python god as well as make their final transition into womanhood. As they danced, alcohol in the form of homemade beer was poured into the lake. The girls danced, the drums beat, and the beer was passed around our circle of men freely. The more beer passed, the more we talked and laughed.

Until the weaning stage, Venda children run around naked but for a string of wild cotton tied around the waist called *Ludede*. Once weaned from the mother's breast, they wear the *Tshideka*, a square cloth sewn onto the *Ludede* to cover their private parts. The young girls wear narrow strips of cloth hanging between their legs over a girdle in the front and back. The married women wear a ceremonial back apron made of sheepskin called *Gwana.* Twisted grass, *Vhukunda,* is made into bracelets and necklaces for the Venda girls to wear. Old women wear a goatskin apron covering their front and back that is similar to the *Tshirivha* worn by married women.

The women serve the men food by placing the bowl on the ground in front of him as she bows on her knees with her head down until he gives his approval. This was not a custom of neither my nor *Zuri's* tribes but since we were their guests, *Zuri* and I played along. She cracked a small smile when I winked at her and nodded my head indicating to her the food was to my liking. The dishes served were Mopane worms mixed with tomatoes and onions along with Maize and spinach pancakes.

After finishing our meal, the homemade beer kept flowing, the girls kept dancing, the drums continued to beat, and the children ran around laughing and playing. I learned much about the Venda tribe as all the men joined in the telling of current as well as ancestral stories. At one point, the Chief signaled an end to the frivolity as all grew silent and he stepped forward to select one of the Domba dancers to be his new bride. When he and his young bride disappeared into the surrounding forest, the festivities started up again.

The sky was dark and heavily laden with millions of twinkling stars. The night was calm with a soft summer breeze. It had been a long time since we last enjoyed the company of other people. I would have stayed longer but I realized it was time to go when I looked over to see *Zuri* yawning while sitting with her arms around a sleeping *Safari,* and *Nobomi.* Although saddened from not having been introduced to my next spiritual guide to continue my journey to find my father, *Mfalme,* my heart was full of love for our new friends and my family. After bidding the Venda people goodbye and thanking them for their hospitality, a young man readied himself to lead us through the mythical Thathe Vondo Forest and down the Soutpansberg Mountain. As the beating of the drums slowly faded into silence, we neared the bottom of the mountain, To our surprise, our faithful friends *Yatima, Kong, King,* and *Mbwa* were waiting for us. When Yatima dropped down to his front knees, *Zuri, Safari,* and *Nobomi* climbed atop him thankful for the ride home. *Mbwa* led the way.

Just as we neared the hollowed out baobab tree we now called home, *Mbwa* stopped dead in his tracks. Sniffing the air then turning to growl in our direction, his eyes glowed past us and out into the darkness of the night. I knew he was warning us to not take another step. *Kong* and *King* rushed to his side. It was then that it occurred to me that I had not armed myself this night. While I was subconsciously cursing myself for not being more prepared to protect my family, *Mbwa, Kong,* and *King* were ever so quietly creeping in the direction from which we just came and had already disappeared from sight.

Knowing what I must do to protect my family, I ordered *Yatima* and *Zuri* to stay back. Bending down to pick up a large thick fallen tree branch with a sharp pointed tip from the side of the man-made path we were traveling, I further armed myself with a jagged rock. Dropping my red *shuka* cloth to my waist and double flapping it over twice so that I would not trip, step by step I cautiously walked trying not to make a sound. I knew I would have the advantage if I could take this potential foe by surprise.

"Luckily there is a full moon this night," I thought. *"Better to see you with,"* I amused myself with the dialogue from the book Little Red Riding Hood.

Holding in one hand the tree branch that now served as a spear above my head and clutching the rock with my other hand, I warily paced forward with pictures running through my head of my ancestral Waswahili warriors. I would die protecting my family. I wasn't the boy walking with his head down to avoid the attacks of the other kids anymore. I no longer walked in shame. I walked with….

SWOOSH….interrupting my thoughts an arrow zipped past the right side of my head. Turning to look behind me I saw *Zuri*….with bow and arrow in hand.

"Shhhhhhh!" She cautioned bringing her finger to her lips.

"Nisaidie!" I heard a familiar voice call out, *"Kupata mbwa hili nililonalo!"* Then in English and a bit louder, "Help me! Get this dog off me!"

Signaling for *Zuri* to lower her weapon, I ran towards *Mbwa's* growl until I came to where he stood over a trembling man he had pinned to the ground.

"Jabari?!" I screamed in shock. *"Jabari?! Is that you?"*

"Yes! It's me! It's me!" his voice quivered softly as though afraid he would agitate my friend *Mbwa* even more if he spoke any louder.

TWENTY FIVE

Once settled back home and *Jabari* calmed down, I re-introduced him to *Mbwa*. This time *Mbwa* jumped up on him licking his face all over as if apologizing to him for having pinned him to the ground earlier. Next *Kong* jumped on his shoulders and began grooming him by picking through his hair.

"That means he likes you," I explained to *Jabari*.

King sat sucking his thumb on *Zuri's* lap next to a breastfeeding *Nobomi*. *Yatima* was pacing back and forth outside the entrance to our tree. *Safari* was sound asleep on his bed of soft leaves on the floor of the hollowed out baobab. It was late. I knew *Zuri* was tired so I excused myself and *Jabari* as we walked outside to talk. Since I didn't have a cargo boat, we wandered off into some thick brush to perform our peeing ritual.

Jabari began by saying, "My wife had a dream. In her dream, there was a golden haired man with blue eyes and dark skin who was searching for his father. Of course, I immediately thought of you. She saw you living in the hollowed out trunk of a baobab tree in Limpopo. By your side were two small children, a woman, and four wild animals, one of which was an elephant. She ordered me to find you and lead you in the direction you were to go next. She said that due to the birth of a child you were sidetracked and if you continued in that direction, you would end up back where you started….in Kenya."

It was then that I recalled five years ago the argument that ensued between *Zuri* and *Mbwa* and the resultant birth of *Safari*....*Zuri* insisted on going inland towards Limpopo and *Mbwa* was equally determined to follow the coastline of Mozambique. *Mbwa* finally relented to *Zuri's* wishes and this is where we had been ever since.

"No worries, my friend!" *Jabari* said patting me on the shoulder, "We leave at dawn."

"Dawn it is!" I eagerly responded as my friend and I walked back to the place I called home for the last five years of my life. Although I would miss Limpopo and the Venda people, it was time for us to move on.

Up before dawn, I woke a sleeping *Zuri* to explain to her that we must leave and what *Jabari* had to say. We both knew this day would come. Just as the sun began to rise, *Zuri* was ready. I donned my red *shuka* cloth to drape over my shoulder then down to cover my body, stepped into my cowhide loincloth and leather sandals, attached the necklace of teeth around my neck along with the beaded necklace, cross-tied my Waswahili tribal drum around my waist, hung my quiver with its bow and arrows around my shoulder, heaved my backpack across my back wherein lay my blowgun and poison darts and various other tidbits of necessity, grabbed my *mkuki* spear with my left hand, and clutched *Bibi's* coin in the right. With *Jabari* and *Mbwa* in the lead and the rest of us following close behind, we were headed to Mozambique. After that, I had no clue.

It would take us a couple of weeks to reach the Mozambique coastline that runs along the Indian Ocean. With *Nobomi* sleeping in the seated wrap on *Zuri's* back and *Safari, Kong,* and *King* riding atop *Yatima,* we began our journey. At night, we stopped to sleep taking cover under the lush green leaved branches of a Musasa tree. We had to be careful in our selection since it was well known that Zimbabwean leopards often climb to the upper branches of these trees to enjoy a nap. They were known to pull an animal as large as a buffalo up to its highest branches so as not to share their meal with a lion or hyena. It was the wet summer season so these trees provided us with enough protection from the brief but vigorous outbursts of rain.

I had to scold *Safari, Kong,* and *King* for scaring the zebra and giraffe away from a not far off waterhole. Causing the animals to run, the three of them jumped out at them waving their arms in the air while screeching. After I chastised him, *Safari* promised not to ever do it again but *Zuri* felt he needed more than a talking to. Normally, tribal children are taught manners and the laws of the jungle by not only their parents but by all of the other tribal members as well. Elders play an important role in these teachings as they gather all the children around to tell them the stories and legends of their ancestors. Each ended with an important moral that they learned to apply to their everyday life.

From that day on, *Zuri* made him walk by her side as we traveled. I carried *Nobomi* on my back as *Jabari* and I walked. Whenever we saw a wild animal, she and *Safari* hid in the bushes or behind a tree to observe them. Many of them had their young by their sides. When *Safari* saw how attentive, loving, and protective they were towards their babies, he was better able to understand how scared they were when he, *Kong,* and *King* came jumping out at them.

One night by the campfire under a very tall Musasa tree while we were enjoying a dinner of various plants, vegetables, and fruits, *Zuri* softly explained to *Safari*....

"There is only one reason in the jungle for you to ever bring harm to an animal and that is for self-preservation. First, if an animal is attacking you and secondly for food. You must learn to live and let live. That applies to all of life. Do you understand, son?"

"Yes, mama," he countered with his head down and a tear running down his cheek. "I understand. I will not ever scare the animals and their babies again."

Zuri didn't stop there though. She went on to explain how poachers kill elephants and rhinos for their ivory tusks to sell on the blackmarket. With that, our five year old son burst into tears.

"Not *Yatima, mama!"* he cried.

"Do you know what *Yatima's* name means?" I interjected.

"Yes," he said, "Orphan?"

"Yes," I replied taking him by the hand and leading him to the bushes where we would enjoy our first pee together. As we peed, I told him the story of what happened to *Yatima's* mother, *Hediye,* and how she died needlessly at the hands of a greedy poacher.

When we returned to the campfire, *Zuri* and *Nobomi* were sleeping. *Mbwa, Kong,* and *King* having formed a protective circle around them were snoring. *Yatima* stood with his eyes closed off to the side. *Jabari* was preparing his bed of leaves and grass. Turning, he winked, smiled, and nodded his head up and down at me. I smiled back at him. That night I gave special thanks to *Mulungu* for my family and my friend *Jabari*.

TWENTY SIX

By the time we reached Mozambique's coastline, the rainy season was over and the last month of Autumn was upon us. *Safari* was now six years old and *Nobomi* would be turning two years old soon. My thirtieth birthday had just come and gone which meant I had been traveling through Africa searching for my father for eleven years. I knew *Zuri* missed the San Ju'hoansi tribe and her mother and father but she never complained. She knew how important it was for me to find my father, *Mfalme*. *Mulungu* could not have picked a better woman to be my wife than *Zuri*. I love her unconditionally.

I wondered how far we were going to follow the Mozambique coastline. It would be rude of me to ask *Jabari* or to fire question after question at him. Such an action would show my distrust in *Mulungu* so I kept quiet and obediently followed him. As we continued along the shores of the clear blue and turquoise waters of the Indian Ocean, we were able to enjoy the clean, unlittered white sands of the beach, the blue skies, the billowing white clouds, and the sun glowing down on us as it cast its light and warmth on this part of our planet.

As we walked, *Jabari's* direction and pace seemed to be controlled by a school of dolphins swimming not far off the shoreline. It was when they completely disappeared that *Jabari* brought us to a sudden halt. Before us stood a Port.

"We are here!" he shouted sounding equally as surprised as we were, "Follow me!"

Laughing, I shouted back at him, "That's what we've been doing."

We were at the entrance to the Port of Maputo. The heavy clanging sounds of forklifts and pay loaders filled the air as they busily whirred their way around the Port grounds loading and unloading cargo onto and off designated ships. When we walked onto the level where the cargo boats were docked, men in yellow and green light reflective jackets carrying walkie talkies and wearing hardhats busily supervised the machines and their drivers. When we reached one particular cargo ship, my mouth dropped open as did *Jabari's*. He was obviously as surprised as I was. It was the same boat I stowed away on and *Jabari* served as a deckhand on when I first began my journey from the Port of New Orleans.

"Chacha!" Jabari hollered out to me while signaling with his hand for the others to stay behind, "Come with me!"

When we climbed up the white metal stairway at the rear of the ship, it not only led us to the main deck but to an all too familiar orange steel freefall lifeboat as well. My mind quickly remembered my friend the mouse, *Panya Rafiki*....then the storm, the Pirates, and the ultimate kindness of the Captain and his crew. I had learned so much about life since then.

"Aha!" I heard the baritone hoarse voice of the Captain yell, *"Jabari! Chacha!* What brings you here?"

Shaking his hand, I shrugged my shoulders as *Jabari* took over the conversation. He told the Captain about his wife's dream and how the night before we left Limpopo, he dreamed about how a school of dolphins swimming in the Indian Ocean off the coast in Mozambique would lead us to where we were to go next. Since the Captain felt that he owed me his life, he told us to board the ship and he would take us wherever we felt we should go.

Explaining to him that there were *others* with us, he said without hesitation, "Bring them aboard!"

"There is only one problem," I cautioned him, "Besides my wife, two children, and *Jabari,* there are two chacma baboons, an African Wild Dog, and an elephant."

"Hmmmm," he said rubbing his neatly trimmed beard with his hand, "An elephant you say? And two baboons and an African Wild Dog?"

"Yes, sir," I responded not sure what his decision was going to be.

"And you have no idea which way we are to go or where we are to end up?"

"Yes, sir," I responded once again. "I only know I am being guided by the god *Mulungu* on my journey to find my father, *Mfalme."*

With that, *Jabari* pulled the Captain aside. I could not hear what they were saying because they were whispering but according to their hand and arm gestures it did not look like it was going in my favor. The Captain was a white man with an Australian accent. I doubt he believed in *Mulungu.*

When they finally returned to where I was standing, surprisingly *Jabari* and the Captain both threw their arms around me.

"Give us a few minutes to prepare a place on the boat for your….um….friends and for me to talk to my crew to see if they are up for such an adventure," the Captain heartily responded.

I was overjoyed. Thanking him profusely, I ran out to tell *Zuri* the good news. *Jabari* would later confide in me that the Captain was a man of no religion but he believed in friends, home, family, and repaying his debt to those who had a hand in saving his life.

It wasn't long that a huge steel cage was hoisted aboard the boat. This is where *Yatima, Kong, King,* and *Mbwa* would stay for the duration of our journey. We were to set sail at dawn the following morning at which time *Yatima* would be lifted to the main level of the boat using a wet hoist, thick rope, and a crane. *Kong, King,* and *Mbwa* would be allowed to board via a side ramp with *Zuri, Safari, Nobomi,* and me but once on board they would join *Yatima* in the steel cage. The Captain made it clear that it would be up to me to see to the welfare of the animals….which meant feeding them and cleaning up after them in the way of urine and defecation. I didn't think I would be able to find a large enough plastic bag to store such eliminations of the body similar to the ones I used when I stowed away on this boat ten years ago. The Captain readily accepted *Jabari's* offer for him and me to join his crew on this voyage. In exchange for our services, he offered us three meals a day and a place to sleep. We readily accepted.

That evening, I ventured into the city to purchase hay, bananas, and other oddities that wild animals might eat. I bought canned dog food for *Mbwa* hoping he would like it. The hay would be delivered to the boat that evening. When I was done shopping, I realized that my savings were now depleted. Other than some left over change and *Bibi's* coin, the pocket inside my backpack where I kept my money was empty.

That night we slept beneath the trees in a forested area just beyond Port Maputo. *Jabari* chose to stay on the boat. With *Yatima* standing over us with his trunk resting on *Kong's* head, *King* and *Nobomi* sucking their thumbs while cradled in a sleeping *Zuri's* arms, and *Mbwa* with his head laying on *Safari's* legs, I laid myself down next to *Zuri* after making sure my *mkuki* was within quick reach. Before closing my eyes, I thanked *Mulungu* for making this journey possible.

TWENTY SEVEN

As we prepared to cast off, *Yatima, Kong* and *King* were settled as comfortably as possible in the steel cage afforded them by the Captain. *Zuri* and the children planned on staying with them initially so as to provide them with a sense of safety. *Jabari* and I would make sure they were fed a few times a day and the inside of the cage was swept and mopped vigorously several times throughout the day and night. The Captain ran a clean ship.

Sadly, *Mbwa* decided to stay behind. In the early morning hours on the day we were to leave, he accompanied us to the boat dock but when we went to walk up the side ramp he walked over to *Safari* and licked his hand as if to say goodbye. They had become great friends as they ran, played, and hunted together over the past few years. *Safari* bent down on his knees hugging this wild dog who had become his protector, confidante, and best friend.

"Come with me, *Mbwa,*" he said trying to hold back the tears.

Mbwa sat very still for a while gently licking *Safari's* face while nestling his head into his shoulder. Then, as though he knew if he waited any longer he would stay, he turned around and ran as fast as he could without looking back disappearing beyond the forest's edge.

Unable to control himself any longer, *Safari* ran into his mother's arms. I know he thought he disappointed me because I taught him to always be brave like a Waswahili warrior. But I missed *Mbwa,* too. He was a part of our tribe. I knelt down next to my son and cried with him to show him there is no shame in loving someone. That's when *Zuri* began to sob as *Yatima* bellowed a moanful trumpet and *Kong* and *King* jumped up and down screeching. In the distance, we heard the distinctive high pitched howlings of a pack of African Wild Dogs. Ever since *Mbwa* joined us there were signs that his pack was never far off. At night when he lay next to a sleeping *Safari,* I often saw the eyes of other wild dogs glowing in the dark not far off whether it was at the edge of a forest, just beyond the confines of a cave, or within a vacant baobab tree trunk.

With the smell of the salt in the ocean air filling my nostrils, I stood in the crowsnest situated at the top of the highest mast with binoculars in hand ready to warn the captain of any danger that may be coming our way….or we may be headed for. As our ship chugged its way slowly from the dock, I felt my skin redden as a blusterous wind whipped against my face and the anticipation of being at sea filled my very soul. If I believed in reincarnation, I would have swore I was a free spirited seagoing man in a past life.

Then, when just a few hundred feet from the dock, through my binoculars I saw something that caused me to ring the alarm bell several times. All of the crew, including the Captain, came running out to the main deck to see what all the fuss was about. We surely were not far enough out to sea to be attacked by pirates or to be going at a speed fast enough to collide with another ship. I tried to shout to them but they could not hear me. Stepping as fast as I could down the steel stairway that led to and from the crowsnest, I finally landed on the main deck out of breath and gasping for air. Since speaking at this point was impossible, I dragged myself to the stern of the boat and pointed at what I saw in the water. At that point, *Jabari* threw off his shoes and dived into the clear turquoise depths of the Indian Ocean. When he resurfaced, he had a wild dog in his arms. It was *Mbwa!* After tossing out a rope to *Jabari,* we were able to pull them both safely onto the main deck of the boat. The first thing *Mbwa* did after shaking himself dry was to run to *Safari* licking his face all over while yelping, tweeting, and snorting those funny sounds he makes.

The entire crew laughed and clapped their hands, including the Captain. As *Mbwa* and *Safari* walked off towards the cage side by side, *Jabari* stood in front of us soaking wet and grinning an ear to ear smile that exposed all of his whiter than white crooked teeth.

It wasn't long and we were off again. I climbed the stairway to the crowsnest with binoculars in hand quickly noting that the farther from shore we chugged, the more distant the howlings of *Mbwa's* pack became until they were gone all together.

The Captain stood at the helm while *Jabari* instructed him in the direction he felt we should go. The Captain followed his orders without question. When we were far enough from shore and in much deeper water, the boat's speed was increased to 23 knots/hour. Compliments of one of the crew, I had a small handheld compass to help me ascertain which direction we were headed. As the coastline faded out of sight, we continued steadily in a southeasterly direction.

The crew working on the main deck below were singing a sea shanty as their voices rang out in random baritones and tenors….

"Blow The Man Down

Oh, blow the man down, bullies, blow the man down

Way aye blow the man down…."

Suddenly interrupting the crew's chorus and bringing their unfinished shanty to an abrupt halt, *Jabari's* voice with a great deal of excitement hollered out for all to hear….

"THAR YEYE MAKOFI!"

Then, brief seconds later standing on the bow pointing his finger in the direction we were to look so that we may lay witness to that which caused him such excitement, his voice once again echoed loudly throughout the universe….

"THAR SHE BLOWS!"

As I focused my binoculars on the object of Jabari's exhilaration, I saw a black and white orca, otherwise known as a killer whale, pushing himself up from out of the water and into the air while spouting a geyser of excess water that had accumulated around the blowhole sitting in the top of his head. As he led us further and further out to sea, we were soon joined by three more orcas….one on each side of the boat and another bringing up the rear. I figured that *Mulungu* wasn't taking any chances of me going off course a second time.

Often throughout the day and into the night, *Jabari* and I took pee breaks over the rear of the boat like we did when I was a stowaway. *Safari* even joined us a few times. It gave us an opportunity to engage in a male bonding ritual of sorts I suppose. Since I was raised through the foster system and never had any sort of father figure in my life, it was important to me that I maintain a close loving relationship with my son. An African Waswahili tribal boy is taught how to be a man by not only his father but by the elders as well as the other male members of the tribe. It is a group effort and taken very seriously. In our case, however, since I am the only human adult male in our tribe and I am *Safari's* father, it has become my responsibility to teach him everything a boy needs to know as he progresses through the different stages of his life. Although it is not common for women to partake in these male teachings, *Zuri* was a great help to me as her knowledge came from not only living amongst her people but to have studied in a formal school system as well. In the Waswahili tribe, when a boy reaches a certain age, his rite of passage into manhood involves him standing stoically without flinching or making a sound while being circumcised without any form of anesthetic. I was determined that *Safari* would be introduced to the rituals, traditions, and ways of life of the Waswahili just as he would have if we lived with my father's tribe. I wanted him to experience no confusion or major changes in his life when I found my father, *Mfalme.* If what I was told was true that my grandfather had not succumb to the ways of modern man and their religions, then his tribe was among the few remaining aboriginal tribes and he was living as he was born to live. A sense of pride swept over me as I dropped to my knees to give thanks to *Mulungu* and those he supplied with the *mana* necessary to guide me on this journey.

After feeding *Yatima, Kong, King,* and *Mbwa* the first evening aboard the cargo ship, I gathered *Zuri, Safari,* and *Nobomi* to accompany me in joining the Captain and his crew in the dining area to enjoy a hot meal along with an allotted amount of alcohol in the way of one glass of wine or one bottle of beer. Much laughter ensued as each crew member told his version of the story of how a stowaway once saved them from being taken captive and held for ransom by a band of Somali pirates.

That night, before retiring to our cabin, *Safari* and *Nobomi* had great fun showering. Since they were accustomed to bathing at the bank of a river or beneath a waterfall, the shower was a source of modern technology to which they had not been introduced. It didn't take long for them to start clapping their hands beneath the warm soothing water vigorously pouring down from the shower spout above their heads. Then, children being children, they found a way to capture a small amount of water in their cupped hands and douse the other with it. Neither wanted to stop but it was getting late and another invention from the modern world awaited us in our cabin….a bed, complete with a mattress, soft pillows, and warm blankets. I worried that these luxuries might spoil them but *Zuri,* having lived in the city at one time, thought they would make them appreciate the lives of freedom they were born into more as it did her. Before closing my eyes to sleep, I prayed to *Mulungu* to also guide my children down the right paths through their lives.

As the sounds of the ship's engines and the lapping of water on the ship's sides lulled me to sleep, I felt myself sinking deeper and deeper into the unknown world of the Ocean's depths as I began to dream....

The water was warm. Strangely, I was able to breathe. As my body's gravity gave in to the ebb and flow of the ocean water surrounding me, I soon learned how to navigate myself. I walked, swam, ran, and floated with the greatest of ease and agility. Swimming with the likes of a variety of fish while admiring the beauty of the different colorful shells and corals that sat stationary on the ocean floor, I remained in a state of awe for several minutes....or more. It suddenly occurred to me that time was nonexistent as I watched a giant tortoise gracefully swim past me paying me no mind at all....as though I did not exist or as though my presence was not only normal but expected as well. Soon I noticed his return only to swim around me over and over again....as though he wanted my attention. At one point, he gently swam under me so that I would be positioned to ride on his back. I could have swore he was smiling. All at once, a six foot long shark came into view with his mouth wide open and his sharp jagged teeth salivating for a bite of me. When he was right up on us, the tortoise disappeared and....

I woke up! My heart was beating a million beats per minute, sweat was pouring down my face as I panted and gasped for air. I quickly looked around the room in an attempt to locate *Zuri, Safari, and Nobomi*....who thankfully were all sleeping soundly and safely in their beds. Beneath the blankets on *Safari's* bed, I saw a dog's tail sticking out. *Safari* must have snuck *Mbwa* out of the cage and into his bed when everyone was sleeping. I would talk to him about that tomorrow. I rushed up to the main deck to check on *Yatima, Kong,* and *King. King* was sucking his thumb as he lay sleeping peacefully in *Kong's* arms while *Yatima* stood over them as he balanced his tall stature and heavy weight easily swaying to the motion of the ship.

Walking to the front of the ship, the moon was full and millions of stars lit up the darkness of night. I stood in awe as we diligently followed the killer whale while he effortlessly lead us across the Indian Ocean to whatever destination we were headed. I decided to name him *Nyangumi,* which is Kiswahili for whale. The whale on the *right* side of the ship I named *Haki,* the one on the *left Kusho* and the one in the *rear Nyuma.* Each name was representative of their position in relation to the cargo ship.

Upon my return to our cabin, I found everyone to be sleeping. Taking a moment to pull the blanket down to cover *Mbwa's* wagging tail and to softly kiss each of my children on the forehead, I then scrunched myself in next to a sleeping *Zuri.* Cradling her in my arms, I fell into a peaceful dreamless sleep.

TWENTY EIGHT

The next morning I awoke to the turbulent tilting of the ship as it was thrust back and forth and from side to side. Strong gusts of wind powerfully pushed their way from bow to stern, port to starboard, and up and down the hallways voicing their anger in hauntingly hollow roars and hisses. I figured by now we had been traveling in a southeasterly direction for over twenty-four hours. At 23 knots/hr, we were well out to sea....perhaps as far as six hundred miles....or more. Running up the stairs to the main deck, I hurried onward to the bow where I was greeted by a mammoth sized swell as it plunged itself over the bow heaving me several feet backwards to the floor. *Jabari* and the Captain were on the completely enclosed bridge at the front of the ship. Modern technology was never more apparent in the way of various computerized systems standing side by side all along the windowed room. One of the crew was standing at the helm in the middle of the room. Another crew member stood scanning the horizon with a pair of binoculars.

"The Indian Ocean can be a dangerous lady. Many a man has been grabbed up into her swells never to be seen again. Keep the little ones below deck for now." the Captain hollered out even though he was standing right next to me.

"Where is *Nyangumi?*" I asked.

"Who is *Nyangumi?*" he shouted in response to my question all the while keeping his eyes straight forward.

"The whale!" I responded. "That's what I named him. It is Kiswahili for *Whale.*"

The Captain nodded his head *Jabari's* way as though he had more important things to do than continue this conversation with me. *Jabari* pointed to a radar screen that voiced a continuous evenly paced beeping sound.

"This is a Sonar Sound System," he said as though he was an expert on it.

"Does it keep track of the whale that has been leading us to wherever we are headed?" I asked having read a bit on sonar systems when I was back in the States.

"Yeah! That's right!" he exclaimed as the ship suddenly took a hard hit from a sixteen foot swell to its starboard (right) side.

"It's a little more complicated than that but in a nutshell that's a good explanation." the Captain laughed as he instructed the helmsman to right the ship back to a level position.

If I didn't know better I would have thought the Captain was actually enjoying the ride. He looked to be well into his fifties. He was a bit overweight. Stout is what I would call him. A rebel of sorts I imagined as he wore his mostly grey hair back in a short ponytail….hardly recognizable actually when tucked beneath his hat. An only child. He came from a wealthy family who made their money off of cargo shipping. They were said to own a fleet of cargo boats to which he would one day be heir. He was about an inch shorter than me which always made me feel better when I stood next to him. He had a bulbous nose….I supposed from having one drink too many back in the day.

214

His overly puffy cheeks were chafed and reddened from having been beaten on one too many times by the sea winds. He spoke with an Australian accent. I was told his wife and two children were killed in a motor vehicle accident several years ago and he has dedicated his life to the sea ever since. It is said that the last time he stepped foot on land was when he attended his family's burial.

All at once, I remembered *Yatima, Kong,* and *King.* I supposed *Mbwa* was still back in bed with *Safari.*

"I have to go check on the animals!" I shouted to *Jabari.*

"They should be okay," he shouted back cupping his hands to his mouth in an attempt to form a megaphone shape. "I threw a tarp over the cage and secured it to the floor so it won't flap around in the wind."

"Asante rafiki yangu." I said thanking my friend.

"You're welcome my friend," he replied smiling that wide grin while nodding his head.

Struggling to maintain my balance, I made my way towards the cage. The tarp *Jabari* secured was solidly in place. After locating the entry gate, I made sure the covering was still intact when I entered.

To my surprise, *Yatima* was laying down. Peeking over his back was *Kong.* In another corner sat *Zuri, Nobomi,* and *King.* Along with *Nobomi, King* was nestled in *Zuri's* arms. They were both sucking their thumbs. *Zuri* was singing a soothing song to all of them in Kiswahili. In the front of them nearest to the entryway sat *Safari* with my tribal drum between his legs. At his side lay *Mbwa.*

215

I stood quietly as I listened to *Zuri's* soft comforting voice as it blended in with the beat *Safari* was playing on the tribal drum. Soon I was swept into a world of no fear. If the swells continued to batter against the sides of the cargo ship, I was no longer aware. Staring at *Safari* as his hands and fingers adeptly beat on the tribal drum with his eyes closed, I noticed the peaceful smile on his face. I knew he had transcended to another place and time and would not return until the music ended.

Zuri's calming voice continued singing….

"Lala mtoto lala lala lala lala
(Sleep child sleep, sleep sleep sleep)
Lala sinzia lala
(Sleep slumber sleep)
Lala mpendwa lala lala lala lala
(Sleep beloved sleep, sleep sleep sleep)
Lala sinzia lala
(Sleep slumber sleep)

Jua nalo limezama
(The sun has also set)
Lala sinzia lala
(Sleep slumber sleep)
Ndege wote wamelala
(All the birds are asleep)
Lala sinzia lala
(Sleep slumber sleep)

Lala mtoto lala lala lala lala
(Sleep child sleep, sleep sleep sleep)
Lala sinzia lala
(Sleep slumber sleep)

Mama baba wakupenda
(Dad and mum loves you)
Lala sinzia lala
(Sleep slumber sleep)
Bibi baba wakupenda
(Grandpa and grandma loves you)
Lala sinzia lala
(Sleep slumber sleep)

Lala mtoto lala lala lala lala
(Sleep child sleep, sleep sleep sleep)
Lala sinzia lala
(Sleep slumber sleep)
Lala mpendwa lala lala lala lala
(Sleep beloved sleep, sleep sleep sleep)
Lala sinzia lala
(Sleep slumber sleep)"

At the end of the song, *Safari's* eyes opened. On his face he wore a look of surprise.

"*Baba!*" he yelled running to me. "I saw *babu Mfalme!*"

Sweeping him up in my arms, I noticed he was shaking. Looking over at *Zuri,* she had a knowing smile on her face. *Nobomi, Yatima, Kong, King,* and *Mbwa* were soundly sleeping.

"You saw your grandfather, *Mfalme?*" I asked.

"Yes, *baba!*" he said with a great deal of excitement in his voice. "I went to a beautiful island. There were many trees and white sand beaches. *Babu Mfalme* was crying. He told me he missed you *baba!*"

"What else did he say?" I asked.

"Nothing else. When the music stopped, I was brought back here."

After having a long talk with *Safari* about the power to transcend and there is nothing to fear when it happens, he curled up next to *Mbwa* and fell asleep. He seemed to be content with my explanation. I decided to talk further with him about it at another time.

A few hours later the sun was out, the skies were clear, and a soft warm breeze danced its way about the main deck. *Jabari* helped me remove the large cumbersome tarp from the cage. Next, there were chores to be done around the ship and repairs, if any, to be made.

Walking away from the cage, I glanced back to see *Yatima* now standing calmly eating hay, *Kong* and *King* roughhousing, *Nobomi* playing off in a corner with *Zuri,* and *Safari* sitting next to *Mbwa* with a worried look on his face. I wondered if there was something he wasn't telling me.

Walking towards the sound of hammers pounding and drill bits spinning, I hummed along to the sea shanty the crew men were singing as they busied themselves in repairing the ship.

TWENTY NINE

For seven days and seven nights we battled the unpredictable Indian Ocean storms, rains, and winds. On calm days we enjoyed the warm sun, calm waters, and blue skies. I once read that on the volcanic rock floor of the Indian Ocean lay brightly colored patches of coral reef which were visited frequently by a variety of fish species, including the likes of dolphins, sharks, and whales. It is the third largest ocean in the world and makes up twenty percent of the Earth's surface. On the north lay Asia, on the west Africa, on the east Australia, and on the south Antarctica. I wondered how much further we had to go. Having passed several islands, we had covered around 4,500 miles so far. All of them were inhabited and boasted tropical attractions meant to woo the traveling tourist with heavy pockets all of whom were willing to spend millions for just a few hours or days of escape from their busy chaotic lives in the cities that had overtaken much of the modern world. I understood.

On the eighth day as I stood at the top of the mast pole in the crowsnest scanning the horizon with my binoculars for any threats, I saw it. In my excitement, I rang the bell several times. It was at that moment that *Nyangumi* heaved himself high into the air as though to indicate to us that he had completed his mission. At the same time, the remaining three whales, *Haki, Kusho,* and *Nyuma,* disappeared down into the ocean depths.

Before us from out of the early morning fog appeared an island. There were no tourist attractions or signs beckoning outsiders to come spend their money. There were no tall buildings. No surfers. No boats....other than ours. No pollution or littered beaches. The colorful coral reefs surrounding the island became more and more visible as we got closer to shore and the turquoise waters of the Indian Ocean grew clearer. The Captain was making sure we stayed at a depth adequate enough to not bank the cargo ship.

The sure sign that *Mulungu* had brought my journey to an end though were the hundreds of giant tortoises sunbathing on the white sand beach that completely encircled the heavily forested island as I recalled my dream. But if this was the end of my journey, where was my father, *Mfalme?* Perhaps it was never *Mulungu's* intention to reunite me with my father but to give me the one thing I always wanted more than anything growing up but never had. The one thing I believed finding my father would ensure me.....a *family*. It suddenly occurred to me that it was on this journey that I accumulated a family to call my own, friends were made, and I found my place in the world. I was finally at peace with myself. With that thought in mind, I was sure I was where I was supposed to be.

After bidding a fond farewell to the Captain and his crew, I turned to *Jabari* and threw my arms around him. He was the brother I never had.

"Kwaheri ndugu yangu. Goodbye my brother," we both said at the same time with tears in our eyes and broken voices.

I then ran down the stairs to our cabin and tying my red *shuka* cloth at the shoulder allowing it to drape down across my body, wearing my cowhide loin cloth beneath, stepping into my leather sandals, securing my necklace made of teeth and the beaded necklace around my neck, attaching my bow and arrow quiver around my shoulder, hoisting the backpack across my back, cross-tying my tribal drum around my waist and clutching *Bibi's* coin in my right hand and my *mkuki* spear in my left, I headed back to the main deck to meet with the others. While the Captain and his crew were busy placing the hoist around *Yatima's* waist and getting ready to lower him into the water so that he could swim the rest of the way to the island, I gathered up *Zuri, Safari, Nobomi, Kong, King,* and *Mbwa* into the bright orange steel lifeboat that hung at a slant at the back of the ship with its nose pointed toward the water. When the lifeboat settled itself, I waved to the Captain to lower *Yatima* into the water as we sped towards the island with *Jabari* at the helm. Once we reached the island, we turned to cheer and encourage *Yatima* to us. With his trunk sticking out of the water like a snorkel, he steadily made his way towards the beach. Thankfully, despite their weight and size, elephants are excellent swimmers and it wasn't long he was standing next to us. *Mbwa* yelped, *Kong* and *King* screeched, and *Yatima* threw his trunk back and nervously bellowed....

"Aaaaaaaaaaaaaaalo."

As *Jabari* sped off in the lifeboat making his way back to the ship, he turned to wave and flash his smile displaying his whiter than white crooked teeth one last time. The four of us stood on shore waving back. Suddenly *Safari* turned around and jumped on top of a giant tortoise.

"Look *baba!*" he yelled, "Look at me!"

"I see you!" I hollered back.

And see him I did. My almost seven year old son with his almond shaped blue eyes and straight black hair that hung to his shoulders was amazingly handsome. A round face. Thick black eyelashes and dark skin. Thin. Agile. Athletic. Strong. His heightened sense of survival and independence is what made me the most proud of him. Not to mention, he was very intelligent with a great imagination. He thought things I never even dreamed of thinking when I was his age. He seemed to fear nothing and no one. I could not be prouder of him. He was all I dreamed I would be at his age had I had a mother and father to guide me.

As *Safari* sat atop the giant tortoise, *Nobomi* came running barefoot across the white sands with her arms out and her hands up so he could pull her up to sit with him. *Kong* and *King* each selected a tortoise to ride as well. *Mbwa,* as usual, stayed on the ground never leaving *Safari's* side. *Yatima* paced nervously back and forth amongst the tortoises trying to keep track of the others. I was glad it was morning. This way we would have more time to explore the island that was now going to be our home. *Zuri* agreed.

Gathering our supplies and everyone together, we headed into the heavily treed forest. There was much work to do. As *Safari* jumped down from the giant tortoise's back, he turned to help his sister to the ground. *Nobomi* was so much like her mother….feisty and fierce. *Zuri* took her along whenever she foraged for fruits, vegetables, and nuts. Kinky textured blonde hair with blue almond shaped eyes. Her dark skin was a lighter golden brown than her brother's. She loved to follow *Safari* around. A very opinionated almost three year old child she was.

The Captain promised he and his crew would wait three days before taking off for home….in case we needed them or ran into trouble. I promised to return on the third morning to give them a heads up if all was going well. *Jabari* was to load the lifeboat with gallon jugs of distilled water. He would deliver them to the island, then hide them beneath some mangrove trees we agreed on. Water is a necessity but ocean water is salty and not fit for human consumption. The further we traveled out to sea, the more concerned I became about our final destination not being on a land with freshwater rivers and lakes so I did some research on the Captain's computer about island life survival. If need be, I should be able to set up a system with whatever island resources were made available to me to distill the salty ocean water into drinkable water.

As we walked further and further into the forest, *Zuri* foraged the surrounding natural vegetation for our lunch. Insects were plentiful. The chattering of birds pierced the hot, dry air. *Safari* took it upon himself to climb a palm tree throwing down three coconuts for us to eat later. There was no evidence of nor had we seen any of the wild life that existed back in Africa such as giraffes, zebras, elephants, or lions. We were mostly vegetarians anyway so our eating habits would not be much affected. *Zuri* was keeping an eye out for venomous snakes and poisonous plants. This was all new to us so it was important to remain diligent. We intended to walk to the other side of the island. My compass would come in handy keeping us on a straight path. With only the remembrance of what I saw from atop the crowsnest, I estimated the island to have perhaps a twenty to thirty mile diameter.

We had three days to determine if we were going to call this island our new home before the Captain and his crew headed back to Africa. I wondered if perhaps *Mulungu* had other plans for us and someone or something else would appear out of nowhere to lead us off to yet another location. Just because we didn't see any inhabitants on one side of the island, did not mean there weren't any amongst the trees or on the other side.

THIRTY

It was a hot and humid day. As we walked further into the forest it became even more humid. While *Zuri* paid special attention to the vegetation and snakes, I concentrated on birds, other reptiles and mammals. So far, from what I'd seen, there were several species of small mammals that were mostly herbivores, such as ternecs, bats, and hedgehogs. At one point, grunting sounds may have been indicative of wild pigs. As far as reptiles, I saw a host of different lizard species scurrying across the grass and up and down the tree trunks while *Zuri* saw only non-venomous snakes. Along the beach I recalled, besides the giant tortoises, several different types of crabs making their way through the sand. The bird population was massive, a few of which I was unable to identify. What I was mostly looking for were any signs of human life. A footprint. A broken spear. An arrow that perhaps missed its target. I doubted I would hear people talking, laughing, crying, or whispering since part of our tribe included a not so light on his feet elephant.

After walking until the sun had risen to its highest point in the sky, we stopped to eat. We found a clearing where we could build a small fire. *Zuri* was going to cook my favorite meal of mopane worms along with some other plants and vegetables she gathered. I removed a bottled water for each of us out of my backpack. *Yatima* was busy eating the leaves from a tall tree. I could not get over how much he'd grown. He stood at least eleven feet tall. His tusks were a good three feet long. I was sure he weighed around six or seven thousand pounds….maybe more.

While we were sitting around the campfire, during a moment of complete silence, I heard the sound of running water.

"Perhaps a river?" I thought aloud while bringing my finger up to my lips…."Shhhhhhhhhh."

Everyone stopped eating and sat in a frozen state. Then, all at once, *Safari* jumped up and started to run toward the sound.

"Stop *Safari!*" I hollered out to him, "Wait for me!"

But he didn't wait. With *Mbwa* by his side, he kept running and running as fast as his legs could carry him. When I finally caught up with him, he was standing along the banks of a slow moving freshwater river. It wasn't long when *Yatima* came rumbling through the trees. When he reached the river, he sunk his trunk down into its depths suctioning up water, then shot it into his mouth. The others were quick on our trail. When they reached us, *Zuri, Nobomi, Safari,* and I jumped into the water laughing and splashing each other with cupped hands. *Kong and King* climbed atop a large high rock that sat at the edge of the river bank. When they reached the top, they started jumping up and down screeching excitedly while pounding their chests.

The sun was beginning to set as we made our way back to the campfire. We decided to stay put for the night, then begin our trek to the other side of the island the following morning. We would take refuge beneath a low hanging cliff we came across shortly before we settled to eat. As we gathered up our supplies, we headed back a few hundred feet. The cliff overhang was only tall enough to allow us to lay down in a cramped small space that thankfully was large enough to accommodate all of us. Other than Nobomi, it was not tall enough for the rest of us to stand. *Yatima* stood at its entry serving as protector and guard. Just as we settled into as comfortable as allowable positions, *Yatima* began to nervously stomp his feet. I jumped out of my sedentary position to look outside. After all of the wild, shocking experiences I had travailed on my journey what I saw astonished even me. A long trail of giant tortoises were headed up a small rocky incline towards us. *Yatima* was prepared to keep them from entering our safe haven. When the lead tortoise was within smelling distance of *Yatima,* he stopped, stretched his long neck out as far as possible, then turned to the right and dug himself into the ground beneath a heavily leaved large round bush. The others followed. In order that they all fit beneath the bush, they began to stack themselves one on top of another. Refuge for the night is what I suspected.

"Much like us," I thought to myself as I found turning impossible with all of us crunched so closely together.

That night, I heard *Safari* cry out a few times in his sleep while jerking his feet and flailing his arms all about. Since he was practically on top of me, I became the victim of his punches and kicks.

"Kukimbia *babu!* Kukimbia!" his sleeping voice mumbled while his arms and legs kicked and punched about.

227

"Run grandfather!? Run!?" I asked myself.

I wondered if he was experiencing an otherworldly journey so I lay very still taking the brunt of his blows so as not to disturb his dream.

Suddenly, his eyes opened and he flung himself up into a sitting position.

"Babu is here." he whispered softly looking down at me.

He had the same worried look on his face that he had back at the boat after he first transcended his body. I would talk to him further about it in the morning. For now, I coaxed him back into a sleeping position and wrapped my arm around him so he might feel safe. Soon he was soundly sleeping once again. I could not fall asleep. My eyes remained open for the rest of the night.

When the sun began to appear beyond the horizon, the sky was as beautiful as I'd ever seen. Red and gold hazes blended together providing a protective screen for the day's light and warmth as the sun cautiously began to rise to bring us a new day. So calm. So tranquil. The occasional singing of a bird or two penetrated the air as a warm breeze danced its way about my feet as they sat stiffly at the opening of the short narrow cave. I was afraid to move. I didn't want to wake anyone.

Then, I remembered *Safari's* words last night....

"Kukimbia *babu!* Kukimbia!" Followed by, *"Babu* is here."

I was worried. It was important that he tell me the rest of his dream so that if my father was here, I would be able to find him. I needed to know if he saw any landmarks that might lead us to him. As much as I wanted to let everyone sleep, I knew I could not. Not if I was to find my father. *Safari* seemed scared of something and he was telling my father to run. Run from what….or who?

After nudging *Zuri,* who was sleeping on my right side, she groaned, stretched her arms above her head, opened her eyes and smiled at me.

"Why so early, *Chacha?"* she asked, "Can't we sleep a little longer?"

"No, *Zuri.* We cannot. *Safari* had a dream last night about my father, *Mfalme.* He was telling him to run. He said he was here on this island. We must find him. We have just two more days to return to the cargo boat if we need to. Otherwise, it will be leaving….never to return."

With that *Zuri* scooted herself and *Nobomi* out from under the cave overhang.

"We have no time to waste." she said matter of factly as she placed *Nobomi* on the ground and began to sharpen her *mkuki* spear. Within a few minutes time, she was ready to go fully armed with bow and arrows, blowgun and darts, and her freshly honed *mkuki. Safari* sat off to the side with a worried look on his face. In his hand he held a sharp instrument. It resembled an axe but was made out of a ground down large rock being held securely atop a wide piece of wood with rope. When I asked him about it, he said one of the Captain's crew helped him make it when we were aboard the cargo ship. With that information, I thought better of taking him with us. He was only seven years old. He was way too young to fight….or kill. We had no choice though. He was chosen by *Mulungu* to lead us to where we were to go to find my father, *Mfalme*. There was no other explanation for his dreams and the power to transcend his body. I cautioned him in the use of his weapon....to use it only if his life was in danger. He nodded his head that he understood. *Kong* and *King* were quiet. *Nobomi* stood next to them holding *Kong's* hand. *Yatima* was pacing back and forth. I double flapped my red *shuka* cloth at the waist as would a warrior preparing to fight, made sure my blow gun and poison darts were in my backpack then hoisted it across my back, flung the quiver with bow and arrows around my shoulder, hung the necklace made of teeth around my neck along with the necklace of beads, straightened my cowhide loincloth, slipped into my leather sandals, clutched the coin *Bibi* gave me in my right hand, and grabbed up my *mkuki* spear with my left. The tribal drum would be too cumbersome so I decided to leave it hidden beneath a bush. Walking over to *Yatima*, I stroked his trunk gently with my hands.

"You must stay here *Yatima*." I said to him quietly. If there is any danger you would make too much noise moving through the trees. We must be quiet." I hoped he understood.

As a last ditch effort, I walked away from him holding my hand out telling him to "Stay!"

Zuri was standing by *Kong* and *King* signing to them that they, too, must stay behind....with *Yatima*. They were to watch over *Nobomi*. We could take no chances. We had a limited time to find my father now. After *Safari's* dream I knew he must be in danger.

230

Safari stood up. Looking at *Zuri* and me, he raised his finger to his lips….

"Shhhhhhhhh."

With *Mbwa* by his side and axe in hand, he began to step carefully and ever so quietly through the forest. We followed leaving *Nobomi, Yatima, Kong,* and *King* behind. I hoped *Safari* knew where he was going.

THIRTY ONE

We walked slowly, carefully, and quietly as warriors would when stalking their enemy. *Safari* was light on his feet. He was nimble, agile, and cautious. It was as though this was not the first time he went to war. I knew now that the *mana* provided him by *Mulungu* was the spirit of a fierce and worthy warrior from long ago. Even though his body looked like a seven year old's, his mind and physical essence were much wiser and older. And so we walked in a line, one behind the other....first *Safari,* next to him *Mbwa,* then behind them *Zuri,* and lastly me. All of us becoming one with nature as we blended into our surroundings. Even *Mbwa* mimicked *Safari's* soft and calculated steps.

A few hours later, *Safari* held his hand out for us to stop. We did. He then scaled a tree. When he returned, he urged us to look in the direction he was pointing his finger. That's when I heard voices. Loud voices. The sun was midway in the sky now and I was able to focus on a group of men, perhaps fifty or more in number, yelling out orders in English to a group of what appeared to be the island's natives. They had an accent that I did not recognize. They were dressed in either shorts or trousers and t-shirts. The native men were clothed in nothing more than loincloths.

There lay piled on the white sands of the beach, perhaps twenty in number, dead giant tortoises. The native men were being forced to stuff each tortoise into a large burlap sack, then haul it aboard a large boat that was sitting at the end of a recently built wooden pier. The boat resembled a pirate ship with its massive wind sails reaching high into the sky. If any of the natives moved too slow, a man would take a belt and whip it across their backs making them move faster. All the while a couple of men stood on the periphery of the white sand beach with rifles in their hands ready to shoot at any given moment. Women and children were serving food to inebriated men who were sitting on the sidelines drinking ale.

I knew instantly that the natives of this island were my family. I did not know if any of them were my father, *Mfalme,* but there was no doubt in my mind I belonged to this tribe of people. *Zuri* turned to me with tears in her eyes. She knew as well. Many of the children had dark skin, blonde kinky textured hair and blue eyes. Surprisingly, one of the women waiting on the men was Caucasian with long straight blonde hair and blue eyes.

"My mother, Sarah?" I whispered to *Zuri,* "But she…."

"Shhhhhhh!" *Safari* warned.

He then turned around to head back into the direction we just came. I knew why. Although I wanted to rush out into the open and begin spearing and slashing the throats of the men who had enslaved my family, I quietly walked behind *Safari* following the broken branches and rocks on the ground we left to serve as a trail to lead us back to *Yatima, Kong, King,* and *Nobomi.*

When we reached a point where we could not be heard, *Safari* began running. We made it back to the others when the sun was at its highest in the sky. *Zuri* wanted to stop long enough to feed *Nobomi.*

"No!" *Safari* demanded in a voice I did not recognize, "We must keep going. We have to make it back to the cargo boat before nightfall."

King handed a banana over to *Nobomi.* After she was swaddled properly across *Zuri's* back and the back wrap secured around her, we took off towards the ship. I knew we had no time to spare. The sun would be setting in a few hours. I hoped to recruit *Jabari* as well as the Captain and his crew to help us fight the men who took my tribal family captive. *Zuri, Safari* and I could not do it alone. There were too many of them and they were armed. Again, while *Zuri* signed to *Kong* and *King* to stay behind, I held my hand up motioning for *Yatima* to "stay."

Within minutes we were on our way again. This time, we moved at a much faster pace. I took the lead with *Zuri* and *Nobomi* close behind me, and *Safari* and *Mbwa* trailing them. The sun was beginning to set when we finally made it back to the cargo ship. The boat was in the same place it was when we left its protection two days ago. *Jabari* was in the crowsnest with binoculars in hand. When he spotted us, he ran quickly down the ladder notifying the others. It wasn't long the Captain was standing on deck with a pair of binoculars. Soon, *Jabari* was in the lifeboat headed across the Indian Ocean waters towards us. This time there were several sharks swimming around the coral reefs that surrounded the island.

When *Jabari* docked the lifeboat on the beach, I ran to him.

"There are men, Pirates I think, on the other side of the island." I told him. "They have enslaved my family. They have guns and knives. There are too many of them for *Safari, Zuri,* and me to fight. We would lose and our actions would probably place my family in more danger….possibly even death. Can you help us?"

"Count me in, my brother!" *Jabari* shouted, "Jump aboard and we will see if the Captain and his crew will accompany us. We must save *Yatima, Kong,* and *King!"*

"No, *Jabari,"* I said, "When I referred to my family, I meant my father, *Mfalme*….and possibly my mother, *Sarah. Yatima, Kong,* and *King* are safe. They are waiting for us halfway across the island. We were able to move faster and make less noise without them."

"Kuja twende!" he said entwining my arm with his as a brother would. "Come let's go!"

Jumping into the lifeboat, we sped off for the cargo ship where the Captain and his crew were waiting for us on the main deck.

Once aboard, the Captain hurried over to us.

"What happened?" he asked, "Are you okay?"

"Yeah, we're okay." I responded "but we need your help."

"Come with me!" he excitedly answered as his puffy cheeks grew redder and he assumed a position of authority.

We followed him to the enclosed area at the front of the ship. He closed the door behind him. After I finished telling him about what we saw, he placed his hand on my shoulder, then shaking it slightly, he said….

"I will gather my crew! We owe you our lives, *Chacha!* No good deed goes unpaid aboard this ship! We will help you save your family from these culprits who have come to rob and enslave them. I know who these men are! They are known throughout the shipping industry from port to port and country to country. They are Pirates! Looters! Scum at the bottom of the barrel! They are known to ravage the likes of small tribal communities living on isolated islands throughout the oceans of the world. They pilfer their resources, then leave them to bury their dead and tend to the wounded. Unless we do something about it, they will return time and time again to take advantage of them."

I knew what the Captain said was true. All my grandfather wanted for his tribe was to be left alone and away from those who tried to impose their beliefs and ways of life on them. On my journey, I lay witness to many such tribes who stayed behind. They are living in squalor and having to depend on the government to live. The Waswahili are a kind and giving people but like all the African tribes, they are a proud people. They only want to be left alone to live their lives as they have been living for millions of years causing no harm to anyone and to believe in and worship the god of their choice.

Once the Captain gathered his crew, he gave each of them the choice of either joining us in this battle or staying behind.

"Aye!" they all hollered simultaneously.

Since everyone wanted to go with us, the Captain selected those who would stay behind to man the ship and watch *Nobomi* and *Safari*. I figured *Safari's* job was done as I watched him playing like a seven year old with *Nobomi* and *Mbwa*. We then huddled in a circle making plans to rid the island of the Pirates....forever.

When the moon replaced the sun and the dark of night took over the light of day, we disembarked the cargo ship. Because the motorized lifeboat would make too much noise, we chose to make our way to the other side of the island in the ship's five other lifeboats that were oar propelled. I gave special thanks to *Mulungu* for the calm waters this night. If it were not for the danger that awaited us on the other side of the island, it would have been a perfect night....clear skies, a warm tropical breeze, a full moon surrounded by thousands of stars, the sound of waves gently lapping against the island's shore, total quiet interrupted only by the sounds of the nocturnal animals that live in the forest.

As we rowed our way to the other side of the island, we were careful to make as little noise as possible. When we were able to spot the looters' ship, we banked our lifeboats on shore and walked the rest of the way on foot crossing quietly over the white sand beaches to disappear into the heavily treed forest. Just as I stepped one foot into the forest, I was knocked to the ground by....a chacma baboon!?

"Kong!" I whispered. "What's wrong? What are you doing here? Where are *King* and *Yatima?"*

Zuri came running up to us. When she reached me, *King* came flying through the air landing in her arms. As soon as they settled down, they began signing to *Zuri*.

"Yatima is gone! Bad men took him!" they frantically signed over and over again.

"Do you know where they took him? Was he hurt?" *Zuri* signed in return.

They both began nodding their heads up and down while each grabbed one of *Zuri's* hands and began pulling her towards the other end of the island.

"No!" *Zuri* signed. *"You stay here. We will find Yatima!"*

It was the first time I ever saw *Kong* or *King* disobey *Zuri* as they shook their heads vehemently back and forth as if to say *"We are going with you!"*

Looking back at me, *Zuri* shrugged her shoulders. She was leaving it up to me. I reluctantly nodded my head *yes*.

"Perhaps they can serve as a means of distraction." I said.

"You must be very quiet and do only what you are told!" *Zuri* signed.

As soon as they agreed, we headed for the other side of the island. Time was of the essence. I didn't want to worry *Zuri* but I secretly hoped to myself that *Yatima* was not taken for his tusks. If that was the case, he may already be dead.

Thirty Two

There were twenty-five of us and possibly fifty or more looters. Although we were outnumbered, we were matched in weaponry as the Captain and his crew made a decision to arm themselves with guns and knives ever since their ship was attacked by pirates. I was offered a gun but I chose to fight with my *mkuki* spear and bow and poison tipped arrows. I was quite proficient in their use. *Zuri* refused to stay behind with *Nobomi* and *Safari*. I had to admit she was equal to most men in warfare. She handled the *mkuki* spear as well or even better than me. With the bow and arrow, she never missed her target. In addition, she accepted a swashbuckler sword from the Captain. She definitely was lighter on her feet than any of us. Besides, I learned long ago not to argue with *Zuri* when it came to something she wanted to do.

We decided to split up in order to attack our enemy from more than one position. Once we were all settled in our places, we waited. It was up to me to whistle loudly when it was time to attack. The only signs of life on the beach were at a glance perhaps thirty or forty native men who were sleeping out in the open on the beach. Around their ankles were steel cuffs with chains attached to a steel pole driven into the ground. One man who was apparently sleeping stood guard over them. His rifle had fallen from his hands to his side on the ground. I supposed there might be other men sleeping on the boat. Just as I was about to whistle, I noticed several elephant shaped, beehive roofed huts sitting in a circle about fifty feet back into the confines of the forest. They were difficult to notice because their colors blended in with their surroundings. There were bottles of ale thrown all about the ground. A few men were laying on the outside of the huts obviously passed out from a night of heavy drinking. In front of two of the huts a man sat snoring with a pistol laying on his lap. A man-made wooden structure that resembled an outdoor pen sat in a clearing off to the side. Inside the pen were several wild pigs. Another pen served to enclose several sheep and cows. I saw no sign of *Yatima*. I prayed to *Mulungu* we would find him safe. I could not bear the thought of his tusks being dug out leaving him to hemorrhage to death.

In light of these new circumstances, I ran over to the Captain and *Jabari* to change our plan of attack. It was my guess that at least some of the men were sleeping, or more likely passed out, inside the huts. The women, children, and the elderly were either being held captive in the two guarded huts or on the boat. *Jabari* and the Captain agreed. That's when we decided that I would scale a tree overlooking the huts and the others would creep quietly to wait for my signal at each hut's doorway. The plan was, from my lofty position, to throw stones at the roofs of the huts hoping to make enough noise to flush the men out. Just in case there were more men aboard the looter's ship, five of our men would wait at the end of the pier.

All was quiet as I readied myself to cast the first stone at the huts that lay beneath the tree where I sat hidden. With my heart pounding, sweat pouring down my face, and fists clenched, I began to count to ten….

"One," I whispered to myself, "two….three….four….five…."

Before I was able to say "six" a sudden loud and repetitive screeching invaded the night air.

Over and over again….louder and louder….

"EEEEEEEEEEEE! EEEEEEEEEEEEEE!"

That's when I saw them….*Kong* and *King!* They were each jumping up on down on the roofs of two of the huts making as much noise as possible.

Disoriented, out from the huts ran the looters. I jumped down from my tree with *mkuki* in hand. It was when I landed on both feet that I felt the *mana* of a warrior fill my body. I flew through the air killing looter after looter. I was filled with a power and strength I'd never known before. My heart was not beating fast, my breathing was slow and calm, my hands and feet moved methodically striking deadly blows to opponent after opponent. It was dark yet I could see as though I was wearing night vision goggles. The sound of guns being fired, swords slashing, and arrows whooshing through the air exploded around me yet my mind remained concentrated on what I must do to free my family. It wasn't long and the island's natives who had been taken captive joined us in our battle. They had been freed….released from their chains….somehow….by someone.

Suddenly as I moved with the agility of a long ago warrior, I felt my back being pressed against by another person. I thought perhaps it was *Jabari.* Back to back we fought slaying man after man in our quest to eradicate the evil that had overtaken this island, to destroy those who made it their life's work to enslave, rob, and kill the innocent inhabitants of every island they set foot upon.

They were no match for us. We not only took them by surprise but we outnumbered them as well. It didn't hurt that we had two very strong screeching, biting, and clawing baboons on our side. In the midst of all the turmoil, I suddenly felt the ground beneath my feet begin to rumble and quake. I heard trees hitting the ground and an all too familiar trumpeting that was saying anything but his usual *"hello."* A blare swept through the air with all the might and force of one pissed off elephant. In the next instance, above my head, I heard the shrill cries of two African Fish Eagles as they torpedoed their way down from the sky attacking looter after looter. At the same time, I saw an African Wild Dog tearing out the throat of one of our enemies before he was able to fire his gun.

It wasn't long after the emergence of *Yatima, Yule nzi,* and *Mbwa* that we were able to begin to shackle our prisoners on the white sands of the beach now turned red with the same chains they used to enslave the native men of this island.

From out of the dust of a battle waged and won emerged *Jabari,* the Captain and his crew, *Zuri, King, Kong,* and *Yatima.* It was at that moment that I felt the spirit of the warrior that *Mulungu* bestowed upon me leave my body. Clearing my head, I shook it back and forth.

"If Jabari is standing in front of me," I thought to myself, *"then who was fighting with me back to back?"*

Turning around, my eyes rested on one of the island's natives. He was dressed in a cowhide loincloth. In his hand he held a *mkuki* spear. He was lean, had dark skin, dark eyes, and dark kinky textured hair. Handsome. Neither young nor old.

"Chacha?" he said looking me straight in the eyes while holding his head high and with a great deal of pride and authority in his voice.

"Yeah," I answered, "but how do you know…."

With that he flung his arms around me with tears running down his face.

"Mimi ni Mfalme! Mimi ni baba yako." he said.

"I am Mfalme! I am your father," *Zuri* now standing next to me repeated softly in English what he just said in Kiswahili then….she collapsed to the ground.

THIRTY THREE

"Kuja haraka! (Come quickly!)" *Mfalme's* voice rang out across the island as I knelt over *Zuri* who was lying unconscious on the ground.

Suddenly, the Caucasian, tan-skinned, straight blonde haired, blue eyed woman I saw earlier appeared from out of the trees.

"Chacha!" she ordered me, "Pick her up and carry her to my hut."

Immediately, I did as she said.

When we reached the hut, she directed me to a bed made of intricately carved wood. Gently laying *Zuri* down on a mattress made of what appeared to be the white sand of the beach contained in an all encompassing soft cotton-like material, I knelt on the floor holding her hand. All around the room sat beautiful handmade pottery. Each painted in bright brilliant colors. Different sizes of hand woven baskets graced the floor. One lone badly worn black and white photograph was hanging on the wall above the bed. It was a picture of a young caucasian blonde haired, teenage girl sitting in a hospital bed holding a black skinned, blonde haired baby. I did not need to ask who it was. Looking over at my mother, she nodded her head with tears in her eyes and her hands drawn up to her heart.

"Go, *Chacha.*" the woman then said softly.

When I hesitated and was about to put up an argument, she repeated in a sterner voice....

"Go now, *Chacha!!*"

I reluctantly left. As I walked out of the hut, *Jabari,* the Captain, and my father awaited me.

"Come, son." my father said placing his arm around my shoulders. "It is in the hands of the healing spirits now."

"You speak English?" I asked startled that the father I'd been searching for may have given into modernization more than I believed.

"The bed? The mattress? Pottery? English?" I thought to myself.

"There is so much to tell you." he answered soulfully, "Your *mama,* Sarah, taught us to speak English and I taught her Kiswahili."

"My *mama?* Is that my *mama* with *Zuri* right now? I thought she committed suicide when she was sixteen years old!"

"That was the story her *mama* and *baba* chose for people to believe." he said as we continued to walk. "Our plan was that she would run away from home when she was pregnant with you and I would wait for her by the Oma Valley River in Kibish, Ethiopia. Instead, her *mama* and *baba* put her in a home for unwed pregnant girls where she was under lock and key. There was no way for her to escape. After they took you away from her and she returned to her parents' home, she ran away. Her Aunt, who was forced a long time ago to give up a baby, empathized with Sarah so she secretly bought her a plane ticket to Kibish, Ethiopia."

"But how did you end up here on this island?" I asked stunned at the story I was just told.

"As we moved further and further away from civilization, we heard stories from different tribes of an island that was uninhabited since the beginning of time. It was somewhere out in the southeastern part of the Indian Ocean….about seven days out. The only way to get there was by boat. We needed money to pay for passage. When we reached Ethiopia, we were taught by the Suri tribal people how to pan for gold in the Omo River. They said the gold was worth much money. Then, one day while we were panning for gold, I saw something bright shining from beneath the mud at the bottom of the river. When I dug my hand into the mud, I came out with a big chunk of gold. When I showed it to my father and then to the Suri tribal Chief, I was told it was not only worth enough money to pay our tribe's way to the uninhabited island but a few sheep and cattle as well.

"*Baba! Baba!*" a teenage boy around fifteen or sixteen years old came shouting through the forest. "*Mama anataka kuja sasa!*"

"Sarah wants us to come now!" *Mfalme* said turning hurriedly back into the direction from which we just came.

I noticed the teenage boy yelled out "*baba*" to *Mfalme*. *Baba* is Kiswahili for father. He had blonde kinky textured hair, blue eyes, and dark skin….like me!

"Is this my brother?" I asked.

"Yeah," *Mfalme* said. "His name is *Saka* meaning "hunter" in English. Your *mama* is a funny woman. She calls each baby Number one, Number two, and on and on until he or she turns seven years old, then she gives them a

Waswahili name based on their personality, what they are good at, and what they like."

"How many brothers and sisters do I have?" I asked excited at the prospect of having siblings.

"You have six brothers and one sister," he answered. "She started the naming with Number two. She never forgot you, *Chacha*. You were always Number one. You will meet them all later when we have a celebration in your friends and your honor."

When we returned to the hut, Sarah was waiting outside for me with tears in her eyes. My heart dropped. I didn't know what I would do if something happened to *Zuri*. Sarah stopped me from running inside the hut. Walking up to me, she placed both arms around my waist hugging me tightly.

"Oh, *Chacha*," she began to sob, "I never thought I would see you again. *Mulungu* has answered my prayers. From the day we came here, I kept a fire burning so that *Mulungu* would know the way to send you to me. Each night before going to sleep, I prayed for *Him* to keep you safe on your journey."

"Mama." I said in almost a whisper as though it was the most natural thing to say....so I said it again, *"Mama,"* and again, *"Mama."*

Then, a flood of tears flowed from my eyes and down my cheeks. Suddenly all the hardships, name calling, and trials of my youth mattered no more. All that mattered now was that I was in my mother's arms. I was where I began. I was where I was meant to be. I was safe.

Gently pulling away from me and placing her hands on my shoulders, she wiped the tears from my eyes.

"Zuri has something to tell you," she said staring into my face as though she thought she might forget what I looked like if she didn't stare at me long enough.

Gesturing with her hand for me to go inside the hut, I took one step towards the entranceway. I wasn't sure what I would find. I could not bear to see *Zuri* in pain.

"Zuri? Are you okay?" I asked with my eyes half closed as I walked into the hut.

When I saw her sitting up in bed drinking a cup of freshly brewed tea with a smile on her face, I opened my eyes fully and rushed over to her,

"Why did you pass out?" I asked kneeling at the bedside and grasping her hand in mine. "Are you okay?"

"Mimi ni mjamzito," she said softly.

With that, I buried my head into her lap and began to cry.

THIRTY FOUR

"Pregnant?" I hollered as I wiped the tears from my smiling face while jumping to a standing position.

For a man, I figured I'd done enough crying for one day. Sarah walked inside the hut with a big grin on her face.

"Did you tell him?" she asked.

"Yeah," *Zuri* said nodding her head.

"This will be my first grandchild!"

"No," *Zuri* replied. "This will be your third grandchild."

"Third? But where are the other two?"

"They're back at the cargo boat being tended to by some of the crew." I interjected.

"Cargo boat? What cargo boat? Oh never mind! Go get them! Go get them now, *Chacha!*" Sarah blurted all at once.

"Yeah, *mama,*" I said, "I will go get them now."

Suddenly, I heard a familiar sound outside the hut.

"Aaaaaaaaaaaaaaaaaaaaalo. Aaaaaaaaaaaaaalo"

"Yatima! Oh, *Yatima!"* I yelled, "Is that you?"

"What other elephant in all of the world can say *"hello?"* Zuri* laughed jumping out of bed to have a look outside.

We ran out the entryway and standing right in front of us were *Kong, King, Mbwa,* and....*Yatima* with *Yule nzi* on his back.

My feet could not carry me fast enough. When I reached *Yatima,* I wrapped my arms around his trunk and cried like a baby once again. He had a broken chain that was attached to a steel shackle around his left rear leg.

"Weeeeeeeah! Weeeeeeeah!" *Yule nzi* shrieked as though wanting to be acknowledged as well.

"I see you *Yule nzi!"* I cried as she flew from *Yatima's* back to my shoulder.

Suddenly, on my other shoulder landed a male African Fish Eagle who I decided on the spot to name *Tai* which simply means Eagle.

"And thank you, *Tai* for helping us in our battle."

"Weeeeeah! Weeeeeah!" they both screeched as they gracefully flew away together.

Then, looking down at an African Wild Dog named *Mbwa* who was standing in front of me vigorously wagging his tail all the while making all those strange grunting, snorting, and sneezing sounds he makes, I kneeled to take him up in my arms. While I heartily ruffled his hair, he reciprocated by wiggling, wagging, snorting, and bestowing lots of slobber filled kisses all over my face.

"I thought we left you back at the boat with Safari and Nobomi." I said to a now panting *Mbwa* as I raised myself to stand, "I'm glad you joined us though."

Kong and *King* then excitedly ran up to *Zuri* and placed two keys in her hand signing that one key was to the cage that held *Yatima* captive on the looters boat and the other to the chains that held the natives captive on the beach.

"Thank you *Kong!* Thank you *King!*" I said as they both ran over to me throwing their arms around my neck and knocking me to the ground.

Just then, *Yatima,* tapped me on the arm with his trunk, then knelt down on his two front knees for me to climb on top of him. When I did, *Kong* joined me and *King* ran over to *Zuri* to hold her hand.

With that, off *Yatima, Kong* and I flew across the white sands of the beach with *Mbwa* running by our side. Then, onward, onward, onward around the island to its other side. At the speed *Yatima* was running, it didn't take us long to reach the cargo ship where it remained anchored in the same spot where we left it.

When the Lookout saw us from the crowsnest with his binoculars, it wasn't long that one of the crew was headed towards us to transport us back to the ship in the motorized bright orange lifeboat.

Safari and *Nobomi* were waiting for us on the main deck.

"Where is *mama?*" Safari asked approaching me with much concern in his eyes. He looked like he might cry but he stiffened his upper lip and held it back.

"He did much better than I did," I thought to myself.

Mbwa was standing on one side of him and *Nobomi* was on his other side sucking her thumb. Holding her hand protectively in his, I realized that my son was growing into a fine young man. I was so proud of him.

Kneeling down to his level, I told him, "*Mama* is okay. We found my *baba, Mfalme*....and his family. My *mama,* Sarah, too. Do you want to meet them?"

All at once, the child that he was emerged as he started jumping up and down screaming,

"Yeah! Yeah! Yeah! Let's go *baba!*"

Nobomi, for no reason other than she adored her brother, suddenly started to mimic him as she jumped up and down and waved her arms in the air, too.

So off in the lifeboat we sped to the coral reef lined shore. Tonight there would be a celebration. Tomorrow we would gather the looters who survived the battle and bury those who did not. The Captain and his crew would then transport them to the nearest Police municipality in South Africa. I was sure there was a ransom on their heads that the Captain and his crew, including *Jabari,* could use. For now, they were being kept under lock and key in a cage within their own boat under the watchful eye of two of the Waswahili tribal men....probably the same cage where they held *Yatima.*

Yatima was waiting on the shore for us as we banked the boat. *Safari,* being the "man" that he *thinks* he is, ran up to his at least seven ton, eleven foot tall grey friend and motioned with a simple wave of his hand for him to kneel. And of course, *Yatima* did. Giving *Nobomi* a boost up, he stopped long enough to give his elephant pal a hug on his trunk. Following my son's lead, I jumped on behind them. With the white sand beaches below our feet, the blue clear sky painted with white billowing clouds above our heads, the light and warmth of the sun shining down on us, the ocean breezes coming off of the turquoise tropical waters from the east, and the smell of the green forested trees from the west, off we raced southward. I never felt so free, so alive in my life.

When we reached the other side of the island, *Zuri* was waiting for us. While *Yatima* kneeled so that *Safari* and *Nobomi* might have a softer landing when climbing off, *Zuri* ran towards them.

"Mama!" Safari cried as he burrowed himself into her outstretched arms.

Quickly lifting him up, she smothered him with kisses which brought the biggest smile I'd ever seen him smile.

"Mama! Mama!" Nobomi's sweet innocent voice rang out over and over again. *"Mama!* It's me! It's me!"

"Yeah, it's you!" *Zuri* countered laughing. "It's my baby!"

With that *Nobomi* started to laugh that laugh that comes from way down in her belly….like a tickle thats been waiting to come out for a very long time from deep down inside.

When everyone settled down, we made our way over to *Mfalme* and *Sarah's* hut where we found them busy at work preparing for the ceremony that night. Walking up to them, I placed *Safari* and *Nobomi* to stand in front of me with my hands resting on their small shoulders.

"Safari, Nobomi," I said pointing at my *mama,* "this is your *bibi*….grandmother. Then, pointing at my *baba,* I said, "This is your *babu….* grandfather."

Safari took hold of *Nobomi's* hand walking cautiously towards them. *Zuri* nodded them on.

Before they reached them, *Sarah* and *Mfalme* could contain themselves no more so they went running up to them and swooped them up into their arms.

Zuri and I agreed they were going to be great *mababu,* which means grandparents in Kiswahili.

That night a huge campfire was built on the beach for the men to sit around and tell their stories of our ancestors never to be forgotten, battles waged, valor, friendship, and family. Another campfire was used for the women to cook. The smell of wild pig wafted its way through the air. Each tribal man was dressed in a red *shuka* cloth just like mine. It was worn tied at the shoulder so that it would drape down across the front and back of the body. Their faces were painted in red and white colors. The young men wore their red *shuka* cloths double flapped around the waist as some engaged off to the side in a jumping contest and others engaged in mimicking their *babas* as they fought against the looters and won. This would be a tale that would go down in the Waswahili annals of history to be told again and again throughout the rest of time around the campfire passed down from generation to generation. The women were dressed in red and white grass skirts with a colorful array of beaded necklaces around their necks and in their hair. While *Zuri* cooked with the women, I sat and talked with the men. *Safari, Nobomi,* and *Mbwa* were off playing with the other children. I knew *Mbwa* would keep a watchful eye on them. *Kong* and *King* were riding through the forest atop *Yatima.*

After we were done eating, everyone gathered round as my *baba, Mfalme,* stood to tell the tale of his and my *mama's* love story....and me. When he was finished talking, he called me over to him so that I could tell the tale of my journey. So there we stood side by side as I'd always imagined it to be. *Baba* and *mwana*....Father and son. When my *mama* walked up to embrace me in her arms, I felt complete.

Then, I was introduced to my six brothers and one sister ranging in age from five to seventeen years. My sister was the last to be born. All of my brothers looked like me. Blonde kinky textured hair, blue eyes, dark skin, varying in weight and height....but none taller than me. All were lean and muscular....probably the result of their diet and activity levels. Each walked up to hug me when *mama* called out their name....

"Number two son." she said softly as all grew quiet around us. "This is *Rehema* which means *second* born. He is seventeen. He and his wife are expecting a baby soon." She was careful to place emphasis on the word *second.* Then, continuing she announced, "Number three son. *Saka* (hunter). He is fifteen. Number four son, *Kanu* (wild cat). He is thirteen. Number five son, *Jelani* (mighty). He is eleven. Number six son, *Zakia* (intelligent). He is nine. Number seven son, *Sudi* (lucky). He is seven years old."

Pausing a moment, then looking down at the five year old little girl clinging to her leg, she nudged her gently towards me, then said, "I named her when she was born because she was our Number one girl. This is your sister,

Kia (beautiful). *Kia* looked much like *Safari* in that her hair was dark and straight and her eyes were blue.

I was overwhelmed at the thought of having an extended family beyond my wife and children....and of course *Yatima, Kong, King, Yule nzi, Tai,* and *Mbwa.* Although *Yule nzi* was not here, it did not mean that she and her partner were forgotten or no longer a part of our family.

At the exact moment I thought the tears were going to start rolling down my face, *Safari* stepped forward dragging *Nobomi* by the hand behind him. Reaching out his other hand and offering it to shy little *Kia* the three of them ran off to play soon followed by two of my brothers, seven year old *Sudi* and nine year old *Zakia.*

Suddenly, the silence was broken by the playing of tribal drums. The young adults formed a line on both sides of a pathway that ran from the huts to the campfire. Down the middle walked an elder. A man obviously much revered by the tribe. Strong and muscular for a man his age. Greying hair. Dark black eyes. Dark skin. Dressed in a red *shuka* cloth around his waist that was double flapped over. Bare feet. Red and white lion's teeth hanging by a twine around his neck. Battle scars on his arms, chest and legs When he reached me, he stopped, held his head high, intertwined his right arm with my left pulling me into him barely leaving two inches between us. I didn't know what I was supposed to do so I stood there not moving. Barely breathing. Face to face, eye to eye we stood.

When the tribal drums stopped and all that could be heard were the lappings of the ocean's waters against the shore, the crackling embers of the camp's fire, crickets chirping, frogs croaking, and the occasional hootings of an owl, he shouted for all to hear….

"Karibu mjukuu!"

Then, with tears in his eyes and a big smile on his face, he drew his face in to my ear, then whispered….

"Welcome grandson!"

It was my *babu,* my grandfather….*Kondo!*

I felt so thankful to *Mulungu* for having brought my dreams to truth. As we embraced one another, I realized how blessed I really was. Perhaps, the trials and tribulations I endured from my birth to the day I met with the dentist, *Dr. Nnamani,* were all a part of *Mulungu's* plans for me….were meant to be….so that I might become the man I was today.

Then, all grew quiet again when my *babu* hollered out in Kiswahili for all to hear….

"Kusubiri! Kuna Zaidi!" Followed by, "Wait! There is more!"

Turning to the pathway from whence he came that led from the huts to the campfire on the beach, he held his hand out to welcome three additional tribal members as they paraded their way towards us with red *shuka* cloths covering their heads and their faces painted red and white.

When they reached me, they dropped the red *shuka* cloths to their shoulders. My heart stopped beating, my head started to spin, I could barely breathe.

"Bibi? Auntie Amne? Dr. Nnamani?" I gasped dropping to my knees.

This time I did not try to hide the tears that flowed from my eyes and down my face.

The rest of the night was filled with the sounds of the young men playing the tribal drums while engaging in jumping contests and battle reenactments. The men and the elders drank, ate, laughed and told story after story. The women talked, laughed, ate, sang, danced and tended to the children. The children ate, laughed, and played and played and played. Everyone paid homage to *Mulungu*....even *Zuri*.

As I sat beneath the star studded sky illuminated by a full moon listening to the beat of the tribal drums, the shuffling of dancing feet in the sand, and the stories of our ancestors being told around a campfire, my heart beat gently and was filled with love and hope for these people who surrounded me....these people who were my family. These people who loved me as much as I loved them. I was behoven to *Mulungu* for leading me to a place where my children could grow in an environment where they were meant to grow....without the interference of modern technology, pollution, and violence....with their family around them to nurture them, teach them, and most importantly to love them. A place where they could live off the land without money or greed and where their elders are respected and honored for their wisdom and knowledge.

A feeling of peace and calm flowed through my body and soul as I looked around me and realized....

I was home....at last.

THIRTY FIVE

The next morning we got down to the business of loading and containing on the cargo ship the looters who survived the battle waged the day before. Their boat would be disassembled and its wood and other materials saved and used when needed. There would be no evidence of them ever having been here.

So it was, with heavy heart but with a smile on my face, I waved goodbye from the shoreline to my friend, *Jabari,* and the Captain and his crew. I didn't know it at the time but my friends would make it a habit to visit me and my family once a year for many years to come. They said it was mostly just to check up on us and to make sure we were well. I believed they also looked at it as a vacation where they could relax while listening to the tribal drums and ancestral tales being told around the campfire. A time they were able to escape that which most of the world had become....and perhaps smoke a little *dagga.*

The first time they visited, they brought a female elephant, two female chacma baboons, and a female African Wild Dog so that *Yatima, Kong, King,* and *Mbwa's* kind would not die out on the island. We were all thankful. My Waswahili family had grown quite fond of them as well.

Every two years, the Captain would bring with him *Zuri's* mother and father to visit her and their grandchildren. Of course, our location was to remain top secret....*until Zuri's* father, who is an Attorney, proposed that he do some investigating for us as to who owned the land rights to the island and if it was for sale. In the meantime, we remained diligent in protecting our island from further looters and the like by assigning Lookouts on the north, south, east, and west portions of the island around the clock. Their crows nests came in the form of very tall trees. The Captain left four pairs of binoculars behind. Due to what happened with the looters the first time around, we made sure those who tried to step foot on our island were met with arrows, spears, and blowgun poisonous darts. We even shot arrows at helicopters flying above us warning them to stay away. The word must have gotten out that we weren't a people to be messed with because even when a passing boat is spotted now, they keep a safe amount of space between them and us.

It turned out that the island belonged to India and had all but been forgotten. It was considered uninhabitable due to its harsh weather conditions. In addition to the heavy rains and winds during monsoon season making it an unlikely destination for those who wanted to spend their vacations receiving all the amenities of a luxury hotel, the shallow coral reefs surrounding it were visibly rampant with sharks and the tidal waves could swell to heights of eight feet or higher. Ultimately we were able to legally purchase the island through *Zuri's* father. *Bibi's* coin that I carried clutched tightly in my hand for the duration of my journey was appraised by a *museum in Kenya* for just the amount of money the government of India was asking.

Since the day I first landed on the island where I would be united with not only my Waswahili tribe but my father, *Mfalme,* my mother, *Sarah,* my grandmother, *Bibi,* my grandfather, *Kondo,* and my six brothers and one sister as well, I learned that the Social Worker back in the States who went by the name of *Auntie Amne* really wasn't a Social Worker at all. Her Waswahili tribal name was *Amne,* meaning *Secure.* I never thought to question people in authority back then but in looking back it was a bit strange the way she kept popping up whenever I was shuffled from one foster home to the next. She also was the one who set up my first dental appointment with *Dr. Nnamani.* She is my real life blood *Shangazi* (Aunt)....one of my father's seven sisters. I also have one *Mjomba* (Uncle)....my father's older brother....who turned out to be *Dr. Nnamani.* Normally, in the tribe, he would have been next in line to be Chief but *Mulungu* decided to assign him another job. His talents lay elsewhere. He really wasn't a dentist. His name is *Mganga* which means *Healer* in Kiswahili. He is known to transcend his body in order to accomplish the goal of healing tribal members who have fallen ill. During these rituals, he wears the all too familiar Medicine Man Mask that once hung on the wall in the office where I first met him. He is a very powerful Shaman.

When the elders speak, the children sit on their mothers laps listening to the stories of their heritage and ancestry. All tales are told in Kiswahili. I am thankful that *Safari* and *Nobomi* were young enough to be able to be a part of all of that.

My grandfather, *Kondo,* lived well into his nineties. When he crossed over to become an ancestral spirit, he often interrupted our dreams with his advice. *Bibi* has become a huge part of our lives. The day she walked down that pathway with the red *shuka* cloth wrapped around her head concealing her face and after revealing herself, she stopped in front of me with that infectious smile she was known for and held out her hand. I dropped the coin into her hand that she gave me so many years ago while I was panhandling on the streets of New Orleans. The same coin that would enable us to purchase the island we lived on.

"Asante!" she said throwing her arms around me.

"No, *Bibi,*" I remember whispering into her ear, "Thank *you!*"

My father took over being Chief of the tribe after my grandfather joined the spirit world. He constantly reminded me that I was next in line and diligently began schooling me in his wise ways. I was in no hurry to succeed him. *Safari* will follow in my footsteps. I now have the time to explain and school my son in all of the lessons in life I had to put off talking to him about while on our journey.

I finally got the opportunity to run through the forest hunting by my father's side as I once dreamed of doing long ago. It was just as I dreamed it would be. Oh, what a feeling! We always took *Safari* with us.

Zuri and I went on to have four more children....all boys.

My *mama* revealed to me that the Dorze tribe from Ethiopia taught them how to make the intricately carved wooden beds they sleep on as well as how to weave materials like bamboo, and how to spin cotton. They also showed them how to build the elephant shaped, beehive-roofed huts we live in now. They are made out of hardwood poles, woven bamboo and other natural materials. They are quite large and tall and have more than one room.

Every day I wake up and each night I go to sleep, I thank *Mulungu* for leading me to my family....not only for me....but for my children and their children as well. I have learned that it is important that children grow with a sense of identity and have a sense of pride in themselves. I believe that every person has the right to choose the path they will travel through life to become who they were born to be. I will be forever thankful to *Mulungu* for showing me the way. I also know that due to circumstances beyond their control, many of my tribal friends in Africa are forced to live in squalor and poverty.

Now that I am settled, I have time to think, to ponder the past, revel in the present and dream of the future. I now realize that without my disconcerted past, I may have traveled a different road. My beginning had to start the way it did for me to now be where I am. It was my beginning that led me down the path that eventually led me to my roots. And although the road was not the smoothest, it did make me into who I am today. I am equally thankful to all of the positive as well as negative influences I encountered on my journey that actually began on the day I drew my first breath.

I am thankful for being able to awaken each morning to the chattering of birds while laying next to the love of my life. Every single day I open my eyes with a smile on my face knowing that when I step outside the door of my hut, I will be greeted on some days by a blue sky, white clouds, and warm sunshine and others by a grey sky, dark clouds, and rain. Either is okay with me….as long as I have *Zuri,* my children, *Yatima, Kong, King,* and *Mbwa* by my side and *Yule nzi* and *Tai* in my heart. I am grateful for my *mama* and *baba,* my *babu* and *bibi,* my brothers and sister, and all of my aunts, uncles, nieces, nephews and cousins that I was blessed to meet when I first stepped foot on this island.

I begin each day in much the same way I have always done since I began my journey….I tie my red shuka cloth at the shoulder allowing it to drape down to cover my body, step into my cowhide loin cloth covering my genitals, hang the necklace of teeth along with the colorful beaded necklace around my neck, and slip my bare feet into my leather sandals. My tribal drum, *mkuki* spear, quiver packed appropriately with bow and arrows and the backpack containing my blowgun and poisonous darts are kept safely packed away in my hut easily accessible for whenever I may need them.

Although I have no more money today than on the day I was born, I feel like the richest man in the world. I thank *Mulungu* everyday for all of the trials and tribulations, good and bad, that I experienced on my journey as well as all of the friends I made….but most of all, I thank him for leading me to my family….for bringing me home….and for teaching me that….I am who I am because of who I was.